Tricia Lockwood

Will There Ever Be Another You

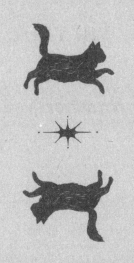

Will There Ever Be Another You

Patricia Lockwood

Riverhead Books ·· New York ·· 2025

RIVERHEAD BOOKS
An imprint of Penguin Random House LLC
1745 Broadway, New York, NY 10019
penguinrandomhouse.com

Copyright © 2025 by Patricia Lockwood

Penguin Random House values and supports copyright.
Copyright fuels creativity, encourages diverse voices, promotes
free speech, and creates a vibrant culture. Thank you for buying an authorized
edition of this book and for complying with copyright laws by not reproducing,
scanning, or distributing any part of it in any form without permission. You are
supporting writers and allowing Penguin Random House to continue to publish
books for every reader. Please note that no part of this book may be
used or reproduced in any manner for the purpose of training
artificial intelligence technologies or systems.

Riverhead and the R colophon are registered trademarks of
Penguin Random House LLC.

Grateful acknowledgment is made for permission to reprint the following:

Excerpt from *Debriefing: Collected Stories* by Susan Sontag, edited by Benjamin Taylor.
Copyright © 2017 by David Rieff. Reprinted by permission of Farrar, Straus and Giroux,
and Tantor Audio, a division of Recorded Books. All rights reserved.
Line from "Gnosticism IV" from *Decreation: Poetry, Essays, Opera* by Anne Carson,
copyright © 2005 by Anne Carson. Used by permission of Alfred A. Knopf,
an imprint of the Knopf Doubleday Publishing Group, a division of
Penguin Random House LLC. All rights reserved.
Jean Valentine, "The One You Wanted to Be Is the One You Are"
from *Light Me Down: The New & Collected Poems of Jean Valentine*. Copyright © 1992
by Jean Valentine. Reprinted with the permission of The Permissions Company,
LLC, on behalf of Alice James Books, alicejamesbooks.org.

Book design by Christina Nguyen

Library of Congress Cataloging-in-Publication Data
Names: Lockwood, Patricia, author.
Title: Will there ever be another you / Patricia Lockwood.
Description: New York : Riverhead Books, 2025.
Identifiers: LCCN 2024057343 (print) | LCCN 2024057344 (ebook) |
ISBN 9780593718551 (hardcover) | ISBN 9780593718575 (ebook)
Subjects: LCGFT: Novels.
Classification: LCC PS3612.O27 W55 2025 (print) |
LCC PS3612.O27 (ebook) | DDC 811/.6 [B]—dc23/eng/20241223
LC record available at https://lccn.loc.gov/2024057343
LC ebook record available at https://lccn.loc.gov/2024057344

International edition ISBN: 9798217179077

Printed in the United States of America
1st Printing

The authorized representative in the EU for product safety and compliance
is Penguin Random House Ireland, Morrison Chambers, 32 Nassau Street,
Dublin D02 YH68, Ireland, https://eu-contact.penguin.ie.

One of us (i.e. a human being) should be imagined as having been created in a single stroke; created perfect and complete but with his vision obscured so that he cannot perceive external entities; created falling through air or a void, in such a manner that he is not struck by the firmness of the air in any way that compels him to feel it, and with his limbs separated so that they do not come in contact with or touch each other. Then contemplate the following: can he be assured of the existence of himself?

—Ibn Sina

CONTENTS

Part One

Fairy Pools ·· *3*

The Changeling ·· *19*

Part Two

Presence ·· *71*

The Artist Is Present ·· *75*

Hashish in Marseilles ·· *89*

Mr. Tolstoy, You're Driving Me Mad ·· *97*

The Wheatfield ·· *115*

Schutzenfest ·· *121*

Be-ing A-live ·· *139*

Shakespeare's Wife ·· *143*

Boys Over Flowers ·· *149*

Part Three

Hidden Track ·· *157*

Life-and-Death ·· *161*

The Wound ·· *175*

Doppelgänger ·· *185*

The Scrapers ·· *189*

Beginning Metals ·· *197*

The Art of Biography ·· *213*

The Ranking of the Arts ·· *221*

Epilogue ·· *237*

Part One

Fairy Pools

As soon as she touched down in Scotland, she believed in fairies. No, as soon as the rock and velvet of Inverness rushed up to her where she was falling, a long way through the hagstone hole of a cloud, and she plunged down into the center of the cloud and stayed there. You used to set a child out for them, she thought, and was caught in the arms, and awoke on the green hillside.

"Sco'land," she heard her mother say, in a voice weak from lack of iced tea—they were barely alive, after five hours on the runway in Chicago and another ten in the air. "It's not the first real day," her husband kept reminding them; after a short stay in Inverness that night, they would go on to Skye tomorrow. He jangled a set of keys. In Ireland, two years before, it had transpired that her husband, a contrarian, was born to drive on the wrong side of the road, while her mother, a worse contrarian—and whom she had defeated by marrying the former—planned to drag them all to hell that way. "So I'll drive," he told her mother now, very loudly, "and you sit on the passenger side and slam your foot to the floor whenever I get too close to a low stone wall." Deal, her mother agreed; she would also provide commentary, and throw in those sharp little gasps for free.

She herself was silent and let herself be carried, on and on toward the green hillside. The trees corresponded to an obsessive high school reading of *The White Goddess*. The sheep were spray-painted according to who owned them. Actual lambs frisked in the fields, on legs like little girls'. Wait, she thought, am I confused about changelings? You put them out, did you get anything back? Or they were taken from you in the night, and you woke up one morning . . .

Her sister sat apart from her in the rental car. Her head was full of the Child, lost to them all just that January. From time to time you saw her flicking through pictures on her phone with a chipped hot-pink manicure, so quickly that she appeared to be alive. As if she were smoothing a forehead, or touching away an eyelash, or wiping milk from a mouth, and once again the whole life was in motion.

"Wide load," she heard her mother saying to the asses of the sheep, as if they were women.

Upon her arrival, instead of taking pictures of the North Sea, she had taken pictures of elk bellowing on the walls and a little guy who appeared to be penetrating his bagpipes. This was her typical routine in other countries, to first take pictures of their pictures. It was how you entered into the spirit, and by eating the complimentary oatcakes that had been left in your room, with its conscious and unconscious plaids: light, shadow, her hand crossed over her sister's, and that life called through-the-window.

Which called them out. She picked up a stone from the shore of the North Sea, with a ring of mica around the top like the city flashing on the water, and they piled into the car to go looking for it, wrapped in a series of preposterous scarves. When she thought of changelings, hadn't it been mostly of the way they were wrapped—in rough gray cloth, with a triangle of face shining through?

Between the time her mother had gone into her hotel room and the time she reappeared in the hall, her jeans had become wet. They would not dry for the rest of the trip. The wetness came to represent, in the rest of their minds, the iced tea she could never get. "Tea . . . with ice?" she would ask hopefully, making a series of gestures to communicate the concept of iced tea, and be brought a cup with three cubes in it by someone who looked almost medically concerned.

"Tea . . . with ice?" she asked at the restaurant, holding up her hands like shocked daisies next to her eyes. They had gone to three or four places before finding one that was open. The chef, in a white hat, laughed and entered her conspiracy. The night flowed like just-struck oil outside the windows; she tried to fix the details of it in her mind. She never remembered the first night in another country—something to do with the change in altitude, or as if she really had touched down in another world. The restaurant, she would not remember later, was actually called Kool Runnings.

Back at the hotel bar, the bartender told them the lamentable story of Irn-Bru. It had once been sweeter, now it was less sweet. There were petitions, and people hoarding it by the case in their flats. She ordered one from him to make friends, for short of that she saw no other way of doing it. Scottish bartenders had been given the opposite instructions to American ones. The taste, a pink electrocution of the tongue, was indescribable—and there was a version that was more so? She decided that if she were presented with a petition, she would sign it. And also support Scottish independence, if that were correct. Maybe now that they were friends, she could ask the bartender. But, "Tea . . . with ice?" her mother asked him, and the chance was gone again.

And so that was Loch Ness? She followed her sister through the ruins of the castle that overlooked it, taking pictures of her in empty windows. Her gold hair whipped. Her pink lipstick, drawn far beyond the outline of her mouth, smiled without her. People had really lived here. Could you still surprise someone's breathing near the ceiling, as you could upstairs in her sister's house? How long did that last?

Her husband rubbed his hands. Finally, a country where the women were wearing enough cloth, and where the wind persisted in exposing the tips of their ears. He had turned to pure itinerary; his mind was full of mileage, national parks, famed distilleries, tallest peaks. At this point he believed he was Scottish—everywhere they went they saw bald heads that looked like his. "One of me!" he would cry, pointing them out; a country full of thousands, and she had reached out and taken one. She fondled the mica stone. Maybe the soul was just that dearness nestled in the center of the body, like a chosen pebble in the palm of a hand. When you held someone it was that dearness you felt, that chosenness.

And he was dear. He would sniff the air and stop the car and say, "Macbeth lived here." He knew where there was Red Bull and where there might be ice—three cubes of it, for her mother. In the car they played a game of Would You Rather, except they misremembered it as

I Would Never. This limited things somewhat. Her husband won easily. "I would NEVER do that!" he kept shouting, and then put down another point for himself.

He had done all this to rinse her sister's mind of pain. Pain was one of the things he could not stand, along with muppets—"I can feel them getting dirty"—and receipts, which were endocrine disruptors. "No thank you," he said to the man in the gas station, purchasing four cans of the less sweet Irn-Bru. Keep moving, he said to them, in his long striding body. One foot in front of the other, or die.

She did what she always did in a car: looked out the window, trusted, and let herself be carried along. The easiest life to imagine was the life of the postman. The easiest life to imagine was the life of the man who ran the ferry. The easiest life to imagine was that of a child, in the castle that sat on the shore of Loch Ness—where the water was full, it was true, of little slipping necks. You could just grab on.

They took turns reading to each other from Wikipedia: about fighting hares, the symbology of thistles, which time of year the heather bloomed. The list of historical guys who actually believed in fairies was pretty long, she told them on the way to Glenbrittle. Her husband would have to update her entry to say that she had joined it.

> *'Did you ever see a fairy's funeral, madam?'* said Blake to a lady who happened to sit next to him. *'Never, sir!'* said the lady. *'I have,'* said Blake, *'but not before last night.'* And he went on to tell how, in his garden, he had seen *'a procession of creatures of the size and colour of*

green and grey grasshoppers, bearing a body laid out on a rose-leaf, which they buried with songs, and then disappeared.'

The Fairy Pools had been poured down. The walk up was like the slow exploration of the skeleton of an animal, whose life was reenacted here and there with plunges of crystal water. There were natural bridges, caves heaped with uniform gray treasure, keyholes of bloodstone-colored water, raindrops on the lens, trees clinging to cliffs, the falls too fast for cameras, like fairies, and the long natural stairs that her sister climbed. People spoke every language. Europeans, who knew which laws to disregard, were stripping off their clothes and swimming. You could pose with a Red Bull next to the tallest waterfall and make it seem like you were peeing. A perfect place.

They drank the water. Her husband sat on the edge of the deepest pool, which touched the center of the earth, and scooped it into a survivalist water filter he had bought on the internet. "This will let you drink water from ANYWHERE, in any situation," he had told her intensely when it arrived in the mail. Of course more and more of these situations were arising. As a child she had watched Kevin Costner drinking his own freshly distilled piss in *Waterworld* and just assumed it was something she would have to do as an adult, for the world would be different. They all drank a long swallow of the cool clear water, which was somehow inflected with the word *green*. It went clear down into the center of her, through the hagstone hole and the natural arch, to plunge down the stairs of living rock. Inside her, Europeans stripped and splashed. Now we are refreshed, he said. Now we can go on.

Twenty pictures in her photo roll later, her sister's phone disappeared. Her black-and-white scarf and her rose-gold phone, with the Child's whole short life on it. It had been in the hospital with them, in the right hand, always. It had been what the next one would not be, a warm eyewitness. She was holding it in one picture, and then she wasn't, a bald mountain behind her. Her sister's face closed, impassable; there and then gone.

"I can find it," she told her, desperate—she always had. Five dollars in a parking lot, when that was real money.

But there had been a switch. When she went up, the pools looked one way, but when she came down again, looking for the rose-gold phone, they looked another way—as if they were a story that needed to be told in order, from the beginning, without leaving anything out. Maybe this place was like the world—you could only travel through it once. She rolled her ankle on the rocks. An hour passed, and then another. "As soon as we get back in cell phone range," her husband kept telling them, "we can just call . . ." But no one listened. Her sister's sere hair went among the grasses; her head was full of the Child.

"We shouldn't have drunk the water," they would say later. It had angered the fairies—no, not angered. They simply demanded something in exchange. But as soon as they saw what was on the phone, the face, the flicking motion, they knew it was too much. They would give it back and keep only the scarf, which was just from Target.

She fondled the mica stone. It stayed in her right hand, always. She had picked up others along the way: another off the shore of Loch Ness, another while bouldering in Sligachan, and another at the roadside stop where a horse lifted up her sweater to nuzzle her belly as if he loved her. Maybe she was preparing to build a cairn, which in their miniature versions were everywhere. They snagged her eye, always. How did they stand? The balancing of the tallest cairns seemed to indicate that there were properties of physics we did not understand, or else they were overruled by the earth's desire to be surprising.

The feeling that she was not quite herself began as they approached Glenfinnan. Her body went ahead of her into the church, rippling with bottle-brown light. Irn-Bru, she thought. Sign the petition. Her eyes, floating a little in their sockets, went on looking: a vase with two daffodils, a statue begging for money, a historical plaque next to pictures of water damage on the pillars, which at one point had had to be replaced. "Not an easy task considering the size and weight of the stones, and the height!" the plaque yelled. "We never want to see this again." Ha ha, she heard herself saying, and placed a coin in the little plaster purse.

The feeling intensified at the Information Center, where she found herself sliding down the wall with headphones on while listening to an interminable murder ballad. It came to her: *She* was being murdered. The bridge overhead was bearing down on her. The church was falling toward her, with its spire. Her skin, in the bathroom mirror—we never want to see this again, she thought. "Where have you been?" her husband asked, when she emerged twenty minutes later. It was strange to know that when something was really wrong with her, no one would be able to tell.

"Faster," she told them in a monotone, as her husband sped the car toward the castle. Something was going to happen, she didn't know what. After they checked in, she sat with them for ten minutes on the terrace, where the sun was spilling like chardonnay into the spread of the hills. The landscape suddenly appeared to her as one in which she was being hunted. "Good night," she told them formally, in the monotone, and went upstairs. Something was going to happen.

A maid came to the door and asked her if she wanted something untranslatable. Her mouth, pale in a cameo face, formed the words several times. I cannot understand you, she finally wept. Then, as she closed the door it came to her: *turndown service*. A little chocolate in the center of the pillow. The maid was Eastern European, and all at once she felt, like four segments of an orange, the rotation of the world that had brought her here, and she stumbled out into the hall to say that it wasn't the accent, it was a problem with all language. . . .

Bathroom, she thought. I live in the bathroom, and went to press her face against the rug. Why were the Fairy Pools so green, she wondered, and rose to her knees, and ejected a long green waterfall into the trash can. *Shall not mine true love staye with me when I am hurling*, she thought, for she had suddenly remembered about the existence of Olde English. What was under her legs now, what was carrying her to the bed—it was the old mistaken movement of the word *moor*. Arranging her head in the center of the pillow like a mint, she took a series of pictures as proof: She would show them all later, how close to death she had come. And leaned over like a cliff to release another waterfall.

Arugula, she thought. I'm going to die alone in a Scottish castle because people have gotten too good for iceberg lettuce. Then remembered the Jamaican restaurant that the chef had kept open for them on that first night, bringing them mussels and baby clams and the firm cheeks of something that had no name. Could be, she thought, remembering how her husband always insisted she had a shellfish allergy that she would not, or could not, accept. But she kept coming back to the coldest water in the world, that had gone down into the center of her, that belonged then and now to the fairies.

Fucking survivalists, she thought. Fancy cups. Bug-eating. No respect. They think they're preparing for any contingency, but they have no idea. They think regional camo will protect them. They think they're ready to leave the weak ones behind in the woods. They think there'll be *no money*.

Her body was so heavy. The Child was in all her limbs, she was carrying her through thickets and over green hills, laying her down nowhere, or else she would be taken. If she could feel her, as she had never before been able to feel anybody on this earth, it is because she was the right size. Why had no one been the right size before? A knock on the door. A shape passed by her, neatly tied up her arugula, and made it disappear.

Downstairs on the fairy tale terrace, over an exorbitant Scottish cheese board, her mother and husband and sister were all screaming at each other. Her mother had misread something about the Property Brothers on the internet and was insisting that they were persecuted for being Christian. Their show had been canceled, she shouted, because of their embrace of the true faith! Her husband explained that they were Canadians, and Canadians didn't have faith. But she got redder and redder, believing that they were concealing reality from her. It was the Property Brothers, and they had lost it all! Later it turned out that her mom had gotten them mixed up with a pair of homophobic real estate agents. That was the sort of mistake people made now. It was hard to know how much to yell at her about it, because one day she would die. Also she had taken care of the Child. You could only think of her hands cupping the large head, and how one day the Child had let her head fall forward, it seemed purposefully, so that her open mouth landed smack against her grandmother's cheek. They decided to call that a kiss, for narrative purposes. They made many such decisions in those days.

Gossip was the life of a castle, and by next morning everyone knew. "Are you all right?" a series of pale, cameo-faced women asked her, bending tenderly over her at breakfast. Any one of them could have been the woman at the door, trying to give her the mint she could not receive. Her mother, too, looked a little green around the edges. The Brothers, meekly, were not mentioned. She thought of the phrase "throwing up your toenails." She thought of her mother counting hers—though it had been her husband who came in the end, hadn't it, tiptoeing out of the castle at midnight with a bag of homemade pesto in one hand.

A store they stopped into where the owner had decorated his display cases with blocks of movable type; her sister asking if he would sell her four letters of it, but he wouldn't. That was what was smallest in the world, she thought, not atoms but movable type, and you could not buy four letters of it again for any price. "Thank you anyway," her sister said politely. "My daughter," she said, turning away and walking past the case again, where by some chance the atoms actually spelled it out.

"Turn here," her husband said thoughtfully, as they passed a sign that just said ROB ROY. What about him? they all wondered. Hadn't he been the guy, in the film? Played by Liam Neeson—before he made a whole career of his children being taken. With the big blouse, and maybe he shouted FREEDOM? It was his grave.

Everyone who had been there before them seemed to know, and had left coins and scraps of tartan and white daffodils for him. The headstone read MACGREGOR DESPITE THEM, which was even more confusing. The daffodils, her husband reported, might have been because of Wordsworth, who had written a long poem about coming here once.

> *Forgive me if the phrase be strong*
> *A poet worthy of Rob Roy*
> *Must scorn a timid song.*

"Whatever that means," he said, looking at his phone. The poster was two people breathing into each other's mouths. Flashing swordfights. Cows get raped. Land disputes, and nighttime raids, and what looked to be a long male ponytail. "One of the most famous figures in Scottish history"—wait, they asked each other, really? The hand of anonymity closed around them, squeezed. Was it possible that only a name could come down?

Her mother stalked the perimeter, faced with a philosophical question: how to take pictures of the ass of a ghost. "We should commemorate him," her sister said solemnly. A bridge stretched between the place where the body was buried and where it was not, and she and her sister walked over it arm in arm. They peed in the woods behind the church, thereby linking themselves bodily with Rob Roy forever—they would remember him now, whoever he was, whatever he had done.

> *And, far and near, through vale and hill,*
> *Are faces that attest the same;*
> *The proud heart flashing through the eyes,*
> *At sound of Rob Roy's name.*

"God," she heard her husband say, "seriously?" A year later, she would find herself obsessively revising 150 words she had written about this experience: the grave, the daffodils, the peeing in the glen—the church that was just a door in the air—but she could not make it mean anything, and she did not know why. Her own mother had begun calling her *Patricia* and she seemed somehow unable to stop her. Some mornings she seemed true, and then she was I; some mornings she seemed false, and then she was she. And long after that, she could not even read the 150 words—it was like walking a path into a dark wood—or the feeling of madness would begin again: Who am I, what do I do? Could you resuscitate poetic logic, though it seemed to have died? In the story, she had really tried to answer the question—"He was a Property Brother," she said in the end, and put one of her stones on the name on the grave.

On Isle Maree, local tradition held that insanity could be cured by towing someone around the island behind a boat. Oh good, she thought, easy. But local tradition also held "that nothing must ever be taken from the island, be it even a pebble from the shore, lest the insanity formerly 'cured' there return to the outside world." Oh no, she thought, hard. Isle Maree was famous for the Wish Tree, an oak that had been hammered so full of pennies that it had died of copper poisoning. Many things still stood that way, hammered full of wishes.

A certain percentage of the people now visiting Scotland appeared to be sex tourists. Her husband was one of them, and insisted that they stop at the Clava Cairns to see the standing stones. "It's not a full ring," he told them, with resignation, "but we'll take what we can get." The stones were supposed to carry you back in time, but she had hardly laid a hand on the tallest one, to feel neither rushing nor warmth nor some red love on the other side, before she felt herself back in time anyway, casting a shadow to say three o'clock. Cows stood fogged on the opposite hillside, still belonging to the Bronze Age. The sky touched the tops of their heads, like the corner of the ceiling in her sister's house where the breathing still went on.

It was the last real day. It was the cairn she walked into, with its heart dug out. It was the party of Victorians she stared at for a long time, on the informational plaque. They were happy, they had done a good day's work, with pickaxes and cucumber sandwiches. The sun consented to fall, for a time, through the particular patterns of their lace. It was terrible to be a tourist, she thought, but after death you didn't feel like a tourist anymore. You were a current of the air, you went everywhere. Into people's mouths and out. You woke up one morning and said *long enough*. Today we dig them up.

"Oh my God, I think I found it," she said, going through her photos.

She was sure it had happened between pictures, but when she went back, she could pinpoint the moment her sister set them down. Her dark and wind-whipped figure turned away into the distance, toward the foot of the Black Cuillin. Giants heaved above her, and she was small. And there it was: a loose little heap of pattern behind her, and the glint of the rose-gold phone.

"I can't believe we got it back," her sister said softly, spreading two fingers apart to zoom in. When they finally made it back into range, and called the number—it had to be her, her husband was driving, her sister couldn't speak, and her mother's jeans were wet—someone actually answered, as her husband all along had promised they would. "I have it," the woman said, "it's safe." She was driving it to the police station in Carbost at that moment; the Child on her lap, with a triangle of face showing. "I love you," she said simply to the woman on the phone, who understood her perfectly.

"An American would never," her husband said, happy, as if it were a point in the game.

But her breath would not stay inside her, as if it were pushing the wind. *I begged them to give it back, and they did.* There is an Exchange, she thought; something passes between this life and the next that allows you to be here for a while; the Fairy Pools don't look the same on the way down as on the way up; and you only walk through this world once. In her head she signed the petition for Scottish independence; in her head she signed the petition for Irn-Bru to be sweet again. She had drunk the coldest water in the world and thrown it up again green. No one could say she hadn't really been here. In her head she stacked a cairn. In her head she lifted the hard heart out of a grave. The last thing she would do, before she left Scotland, was to stumble out of her hotel, in a straight line like a sleepwalker, and set the stone with the ring of mica in the knothole of a tree—not understanding why she had done it, crying when she realized it was gone. She walked through the world; the exchange rate stood. Everyone must pay.

The Changeling

It stole people from themselves. You might look the same to others, but you had been replaced.

The first line of the mad notebook read "I wish, when I was a teenage Christian, that I had been more experimental with my evangelizing. *God laid a big egg in my heart to tell you this.*" But, "Please don't write about it," people were already begging each other, so she kept the notebook secret. It was rectangular and aqua, like an Olympic swimming pool through which men with Marfan syndrome glided. No one wants to read about any of this, and so she kept it hidden, and wrote everything down, and felt long scissoring strokes when she looked into it, and sometimes a high deafening dive.

She had now had a fever for forty-eight days. Her head was completely bald because she had asked her husband to shave it, thinking of scenes from old books. Her tongue was purple because she had painted it with something—gentian violet?—so that her husband almost screamed when she opened her mouth like a cave at him between kisses. She took wormwood every morning, like a witch from the Bible. And had fallen so far out of the world, out of the human population, that she could not even rejoin them to watch the butthole cut of *Cats*.

Sometimes she sat at the foot of the illness and asked it questions. Had it stolen her old mind and given her a new one? Had she been able to start over from scratch, a chance afforded to very few people? Had it *optimized* her? It had come all this way, she thought, cradling the thing in her chest; had passed through the hands of invention or chance, white lab coats, wet markets, the gates of the zoo . . . to land in her squarely, like love! Ground zero, she said to herself, sometimes, though what she meant was patient.

Her eyes beat dust out of the tapestry until it was bright. Was she "a little bit high all the time"? Had the sickness blazed new pathways and cast light on tangled old ones? To be sure, she had forgotten the multiplication tables, and now felt there was a secret number between two and three. To be sure, there was the rough pink sensation that she was holding Rasputin's penis in her right hand. To be sure, she could no longer remember names—after watching *Baby Doll* she had spent a twenty-four-hour period trying to think of "Eli Wallach," but all she could come up with was "Petite Suarez." So she had to write everything down, and go back and read it later and be surprised by herself. Maybe that was paradise. Maybe she had died.

Maybe that was fine. If she never formed another memory, then nothing could ever happen to her; if she never recognized another human face, she would never misplace another pair of blue eyes; if the weave of her had loosened to let time fall through at a more ecstatic velocity, maybe she would do nothing but rush and rush until the great gold boulder came and caught. It was fine, she had her hands in fresh water, washing. "I'm sorry not to respond to your email," she wrote, "but I live completely in the present now."

Before she learned of the existence of "alien hand syndrome," she had tentatively diagnosed herself with a new illness called Who Foot Is That. The main symptom was gasping when you saw your own foot.

"Has anyone else felt like a child again?"

"I have dreams now like never before, bizarre nonsense dreams in which I'm not me or even a human being. Like, I dreamed I was a green leaf. I wasn't me, as a leaf. I was just a plain ordinary leaf. When I woke up, I was disoriented to find out or remember that I was a human being and I was me. It was very disturbing and shocking. Have had that happen several times since I first got sick in March 2020. Not always a leaf, but always an inanimate nonhuman object of some type and I really believe during the dream that I am that thing."

People had lost their fingerprints, how was that possible? People were up at three a.m., contemplating the purchase of apple-flavored horse deworming paste, which had gone up to thirty bucks a tube. People—or maybe just her—were becoming confused after they got out of the shower and applying large tracts of deodorant to the skin of their face. People had Alice in Wonderland syndrome, and something called Drunk Baby Head, and dark glittering damage to their vegas nerve. People were writing poems about it—hahaha, she said whenever she saw one, though she used to write poems about everything that happened to her. People had Brian fog—oh no—and people did not recognize themselves. People stood in front of the mirror in the bathroom, flicking the lights on and off to see if their pupils were the same size. "My boogers have not been normal for nine months," one man despaired, and, even worse, "I no longer have the desire to make money," said another.

"I feel like I am a piraha, suffering alone in my hell."

The CEO of Texas Roadhouse killed himself, no longer able to bear the continuous ringing in his ears. In his lengthy obituary, the newspaper printed the quote: "We're a people company that just happens to serve steaks." The sentence stayed with her long afterward, shrilling at her temple like a mosquito. We're a people company that just happens to serve steaks, she would say to herself, surprised by the sight of her own foot.

"When I was home, he is reported to have said, I was afraid to sleep, as I was dropping off each night it felt just like that, as if I were falling down a black hole, to sleep felt like giving in to death, I slept every night with the light on; but here, in the hospital, I'm less afraid. And to Quentin he said, one morning, the fear rips through me, it tears me open; and, to Ira, it presses me together, squeezes me toward myself. Fear gives everything its hue, its high. I feel so, I don't know how to say it, exalted, he said to Quentin. Calamity is an amazing high too. Sometimes I feel so well, so powerful, it's as if I could jump out of my skin. Am I going crazy, or what? Is it all this attention and coddling I'm getting from everybody, like a child's dream of being loved? Is it the drugs? I know it sounds crazy but sometimes I think this is a *fantastic* experience, he said shyly; but there was also the bad taste in the mouth, the pressure in the head and at the back of the neck, the red, bleeding gums, the painful, if pink-lobed breathing, and his ivory pallor, color of white chocolate." She found this in the notebook and crossed it out heavily. It was wrong to copy that down, she knew, but why?

A favorite thing of madmen was to draw diagrams of the institution and label parts of it "hallway" and other parts, like, "God's Perineum." She understood why, now; the apartment had been anatomized. More than the apartment, everything that surrounded her. Her veins went skipping out of her wrists and into blue currents of the air. "If you are not yourself," the doctor in her mind asked, gently, "then what are you?" The world, she told him—it was obvious—undergoing an unprecedented bucatini shortage.

William Carlos Williams talked about passing into the body of the patient for the few minutes he was with her and coming out *rested*. That while he was in the body he tried to solve its problem, find its solution. And came out *rested*. (Even, especially, if the problem was not solved?) Perhaps this is the source of the physician's irritation: He is bristling against us, because for the moment he is in the body—ours. Mine, he says. Get out of the way. What else was it that might rest him? That she was lying down, that she could not get up, that it was so dark inside her he could have a whole night's sleep there.

She remembered a high school library, back when she was intact. William Carlos Williams was opening the young girl's mouth. The magnificent hair in profusion, the breaths coming faster and faster, the sulfurous secret in the throat. On that first reading she had felt the tearing of her own membrane, the elastic of some nightgown around her neck. The girl's stubbornness, which was her bodily sovereignty, and William Carlos Williams saying let me in. And there—for a moment, her hand was her own again, reaching out to claw his famous glasses off his face.

Proof that William Carlos Williams was a modern man was the fact that he named his son *Kevin* Carlos Williams. Kevin Carlos Williams! William, fading into nothingness in the afterlife, might go into the darkness of her body while she was thinking about it, and come out of her again laughing.

"Any other symptoms?" the doctor asked. Well, something was wrong with her heart, but it seemed more true when Mrs. Dalloway said it. She reached up and patted her large prosthetic nose. How to say this—that everything felt like drag to her? All clothes, her eyelashes, the fact that she had hands. In her notebook she had written "Even to have a name seems strange to me. Would I prefer to be called something else, a man's name perhaps? When I ask myself that question all that comes to mind is 'Dennis,' but I think that's because it's so funny to me."

No, she knew what she needed to tell him—that when she was a child she had a Cabbage Patch Kid that was not a Cabbage Patch Kid at all. The year that there was a perfect mania for them—stampedes in the aisles, hair-pulling housewives, when they couldn't be found in a single store—her rich and hateful grandmother had her personal seamstress sew a knockoff for her. The dimples in her knees made you want to die. The cloth that was her skin rasped. The stitches that formed her ass crack were heartbreaking—the mark of something that would never fool anyone, the way hers now looked when she craned her neck with great pain to look at herself in the mirror.

She imagined the woman sewing in a completely dark room, the world before the days. Perhaps she was hunched over, perspiring, one step ahead of the law, with all the materials of existence spread around her. Cigarette smoke. The crack of Midwest ozone. There must have been a moment, the bright needle running in and out, when her doll first felt itself to be a doll—just as the dark felt, when Monday, Tuesday, Wednesday first appeared in their squares on that hill. And how it sometimes rose to her now without being there, the deep empty smell of doll heads.

The sky, broad, bronze, was crisscrossed for once by nothing. Underneath it, they were all having dreams of the past. The mind, with no new material, must collage, remake, dredge up kindergarten classmates. In a story, fever was something that moved you along, sped up time or made it different, parted the curtains for some ray of revelation—perhaps that's why the world had decided to have one, so it could have a dream in which *all the people were there*.

"I can't believe this happened to us. To the world," they would sometimes say quietly in bed at night. To Ohio, even, she thought to herself, though we are not supposed to write about it. But the censors were right, there was precedent. The defining events of their time—9/11, for instance—had never properly entered into literature, because almost as soon as they happened they were transformed into propaganda. A writer of the age occasionally contrived to have a character die on 9/11 in a business suit, but there was nothing more embarrassing, though no one could quite say why. Also, the people of her generation seemed unwilling to live in the small dusty corners of these dramatic happenings; they had to fly the whole plane into the buildings themselves. Perhaps the illness would be like that too. A writer would try to have the whole thing.

Now, wandering around the antique mall that seemed the safest place to be, filled as it was with the things of the dead, she saw a framed issue of *Time* magazine that had the burning Twin Towers on the cover. Immediately she sent a photo of it to the group text, but they responded incorrectly, with actual memories. She would not tell them her own—the early shift at the bookstore, the Jack Welch cutout, the large luxurious salad she had gone to buy herself after hearing the news, her mispronunciation of the name *Bin Lay-den*—and worst of all, her mother calling breathless to tell her, "Your cousin is alive!" and her thinking, Wait a minute, *who*? The same vendor offered another framed *Time* for sale. Yes, it was the one with the cloned sheep named Dolly, and the words

WILL THERE EVER BE ANOTHER YOU?

Outside, she had to be outside, had to be out of the apartment because that was the sick body, with its windows still nailed closed. There were now only three planks of the floor left that were safe for her to step on, and only a single song lyric available: WHAT IS LOVE? BABY DON'T HURT ME, over and over. She sat typing on a bench in the lush hotel square ("DeSoto," she said, closing her eyes and testing herself) so that if anyone passed and asked what she was she could point to her laptop and say she was a writer. Her head was shaved and she was wearing fingerless gloves and an enormous Looney Tunes shirt she had bought herself for her birthday, tucking it carefully into her cut-offs so that Speedy Gonzalez did not show. If she looked at Speedy Gonzalez while she was taking her pulse, her heart rate shot up to 150 beats per minute under her fingertips. All at once a chant rang out. "I have to march," she thought, but knew she couldn't stand for more than a minute or two, so she raised her hand in a sort of improvised salute and then fell against the back of the bench breathless. Something went wrong whenever she lifted her arm; it seemed to jerk the heart out of her chest on a short connecting string. The sentence she was writing was about *lingering effects of the virus*, and she had been examining it for the past ten minutes to see whether it was a lie. "I was aphasic," it read, but would a person who was aphasic be able to close her eyes like that and say *DeSoto?*

A crew of construction workers, on the hotel balcony ten stories above her, gestured at the protesters with their paintbrushes and laughed; she stared up at them until they diverted the laughter to her, and her tongue was stroked up and down slowly with the taste of white paint. How long the movie ran like that she did not know. To not have her face—which, even without beauty, it would seem she had been relying on all these years. And that was strange too, wasn't it? That a buzz cut could be dangerous again, that men would slither around you saying *boy or girl*, that Tweety Bird could mark you as a member of the opposition.

She bent her head back to her work, her right eye watering. Did she sound like herself? It was very important to sound like herself, she thought, and added another line that made it clear how much she now hated her father. If she put down that he was saying illegal Masses in Kansas City, he would be arrested, so she put that down. The crew appeared at the entrance of the hotel downstairs and walked saunteringly toward her, their right hip bones connected to their chins with short strings; they climbed into a white truck and circled her as she tried to make out the license plate number, something wrong with the rotation of her head on its axis. They revved the engine, and the string of numbers she was repeating was sucked inside the sound. She decided: The sentence she was writing was true, she would leave it.

Tap tap tap. She breathed deliberately and kept her eyes averted from her left wrist; if she looked at it for even a split second, the whole world would go greenstick. Structure through flesh. It was her left wrist that had broken first—not in reality, there was nothing wrong with it that anyone could tell, but suddenly it was refracted like a stem in a glass of water. It simply did not attach, not to experience, not to herself. She sent pictures of it to people, as proof. But that's a normal wrist, one man said to her in response. She never spoke to him again.

The string jerked. "*Get back please!*" she screamed at a couple who was approaching her, with their faces uncovered and the sun behind. She knew them, or had known them before, and had carried around dollars in her pocket in case she met them on her walks. But now there were no protections—even her pennies might harm them. The malfunctioning sentence tore out of her again. "Get back please, I had it!"

The bench was the same one where her niece had sat three years ago, drinking a bottle of her sister's milk, so the idea of her had traveled into the rosebush in the center of the square and worked its way down under the roots. Her head, too, sometimes opened out into the flowers, which were not roses at all, but something bigger, pinker, hardy. On this bench, which she now considered a family monument, her mother had called one day to say that her father had spots all over his lungs, and the next day to weep that he was *thinking of schisming.* That's how she said it, schisming. "Heidi and I can put it in the show," she had thought; gold Heidi, who was cowriting the story of her life for television. The father character—he could break with everything he had served previously, he could schism. But now she considered the actuality. That he would take off his collar and step down from the pulpit and . . . do what? Open up his robes to reveal his terrible X-rays? Maybe he had had it, she thought. Maybe she was jealous, because he had a picture of his lungs and she didn't.

Oh she could see those beautiful lungs, with the spots all hung like apples.

A palm lay in the middle of the street like something Catholic, and the spires of the cathedral rose behind her head like horns. When she had first fallen ill, she felt herself walking with Heidi through the hallways of the script, all of it lit by the new flaming of her fictional pathways. They were in each other's minds as they were on the telephone, finishing each other's sentences and visiting the set of the past; if you called up all the rooms you could see what might happen in them. They held hands and Heidi was telling her again about broken dialogue, which is the way things were written now in order to be true.

"But that isn't how we talk," she had almost cried; her people spoke in complete sentences, even in complete paragraphs, monologues, and now, "Um . . . well, honey . . . your father is—thinking of Schisming?"

She re-tucked her shirt. Nothing that serious, she knew, could be happening to the body of a person wearing a Looney Tunes T-shirt.

No one knew what to wear anymore anyway; the street-fashion girls had wilted, the art students had all gone home, and there were never any more amateur photo shoots in the back alley, parasols twirling against oystershell walls. The European tourists were quarantined, in their apartments and their better-fitting pants. The yellow-fever cemetery was empty of all but the dead. The scattered crowds of people hurrying across the square had an interrupted look, as if they had just stepped out of their houses—their sickrooms—to buy a bottle of something that wouldn't work.

"Broken Dialogue," she thought, a light dawning, and smoothed a painful wrinkle out of Foghorn Leghorn. "Honey I say uh . . . I say honey I say uh . . . your father has *Spots* on his Lungs."

The man she knew was stepping toward her with his little red wagon. Him she did not fear; he could keep coming and coming, and in the great dark tunnel would never reach her. He parked among ornamental grasses and cigarette butts, bent over the wagon to have a private word, and then turned toward her with Casey in his arms. Casey was a white terrier and she was dying, she couldn't even walk, and when her father lifted her out and set her down she would drag herself to the next bench by her front paws to beg for something only a stranger would give her. "She isn't ready to go yet," her father said proudly. "She will tell me when she is." They had to reintroduce themselves every time, each apologizing like an old Southerner—pardon me, no pardon *me*. "Pah-donn ME-uh," she tried today, to test her new mastery of Broken Dialogue. "What do you do?" the man asked, as he always did, and looked at her with the craftiness of one who can no longer remember, with his watery black eyes that seemed to have been scooped out and put back in. Perhaps Speedy Gonzalez had come untucked, or her face had gone the high frantic color it went now that she could no longer sweat. . . . Casey rolled under the rosebush, flies in a halo around her. "I'm a writer," she said, and pointed to the laptop, where the cursor pulsed next to either the line about her heart or her father.

In six months she would see him with a new dog that looked exactly like the old one. He would pretend not to know who she was—no, he truly wouldn't know, because he had never seen her face. Her hair had grown long, and she never wore the Looney Tunes shirt anymore. And what was the man's name, she couldn't think of it. Sometimes she tried a letter inside herself . . . *M? T?* . . . hoping the rest of it would follow, like events. George, she would say to herself, knowing that was wrong. George?

They watched disaster movies, and biblical epics—the leper cave seemed nice, didn't it? People brought you cabbages—and B movies where they drove pitchforks into the foaming chests of pod people. They watched a TV movie about syphilis called *Secret Sore*. No, it was called *Someone I Touched*, and the credits featured Cloris Leachman, the star, running barefoot down the beach while mooing "Sooomeooone I Tooouched." The movie educated her husband about syphilis to a degree that was uncomfortable. "I could have a secret sore?" he asked. "Inside my butt, for instance?" "A chancre, I think it's called," she said. "It's the same as the word for ruby." And a ruby inside your butt, she assured him, was the safest place for it to be. The whole thing about the movie was that Cloris thought she got the syphilis from her husband, who she thought got it from a teenage grocery girl. *But it had been in Cloris the whole time.* "Sooomeooone I Tooouched," she mooed over the closing credits, the sound seeming to flow around a great red stone.

No, that wasn't right. None of that was right. The word that meant ruby was *carbuncle*, she realized at three o'clock in the morning; the whole paragraph was invalidated. She went to the bathroom, felt the electric heart shock she always felt now when she saw herself in the mirror, and struck it violently out of the notebook. This was her trick, her only trick. How was she supposed to *do her trick* when everything had been put back in the wrong place? A corundum, she thought, that might never be solved.

Over the next few weeks her husband remained concerned about the sore. "I could have it in my butt for years and not know it," he brooded. But setting the ruby aside with regret, she told him the story of the woman who, when she was ninety years old, had gone to the doctor because she had become suddenly, incurably happy. It was syphilis, which had gone to her brain. The doctor gave her a course of penicillin, which stopped the progress of the disease in its tracks. But there were new paths of happiness in her brain that could not be walked back, and the woman remained joyous for the rest of her life. Maybe, eventually, something like that?

Now a day sometimes swelled like a chest with *something to do*. This one carried them crunching over oystershells and down to the dock at sunset, as—herons? loons?—dipped low enough to skim cream off the water.

They were writers, all three of them, a man and a woman and

whatever she was; they made up little people and moved them around. They sat on the upturned hull of a kayak, which rocked when they reached up to point out a shape in the clouds. Anything could look like anything, could perform a perfect impersonation. "I think you became psychotic because of your Family History," the woman said, who claimed to remember everything that had ever happened to her.

And it was true, there had been the cursed gift of the Cabbage Patch Kid. The Originals came, she found out later, with a signature stitched on one ass cheek and a birth certificate, which is what hers had been missing. Their names were real, or had once been real; they were harvested from 1938 Georgia birth records. If an Original was injured, dirtied, or damaged, you could send it away for rebirth and renewal. *For eligible Originals we offer the following cosmetic surgeries:*

>*Bath only: $40.00*
>
>*Repair or replace an injured arm: $15.00*
>
>*Repair or replace an injured leg: $15.00*
>
>*Repairing runs in the "skin": $5.00 per inch*

Why was "skin" in scare quotes, when nothing else was? The wind made a sharp left turn and then hers was running races, water bugs skimmed over it, dragging raised wakes behind them. They began speaking of their scars for some reason. Well, there was her upper lip, from the swordfight, and her forehead, from the geodesic dome, and the line she had cut in her nipple when she was thirteen, believing the shape of it to be too vague. There was her sister's C-section scar, and staple marks on her father's back and knees, and the long purple lines down her little brother's neck, that went skipping off their bodies and racing in the air toward her. Counting on her fingers, she attempted to calculate her cost; either fifty or eight thousand dollars.

The water reflected her face, which was covered with a thin layer of zinc cream. *The addition of facial dimples. Re-blushing. The addition of earrings or freckles.* There were mirrors in her for other people, flashing, instantaneous: If the woman lifted her arm, hers jerked up on a short string; if the man resettled himself on the kayak, she rearranged almost against her will. If you looked under the clothes of her companions, you would find belly buttons, just like you saw on the Originals, though not on the one that her grandmother's seamstress sewed.

She could not bear witnessing what was between people; great power lines of sex and history swung extravagantly between everyone, crackling like her crossed wire, so she kept her head mostly turned away. Then there was the light, which laid things open with the penetration of an X-ray. They began speaking of their broken bones for some reason. The man, she did not know how she knew it, had snapped his wrist in the second grade, but he was not a knockoff, he bore the real signature, and fifteen dollars in the grand scheme of things was nothing.

The sun dipped lower, and they began speaking of Tolstoy for some reason. The wind was dragging her by the scalp now, too fast, and instead of speaking of Anna Karenina as she intended, turning and turning like a doll in her ballgown, she began speaking of Ivan Ilyich. "The time of Ivan Ilyich's life that was unbearable was not the three days spent screaming, but the years when he was a magistrate. The time when you first understand Ivan Ilyich is going to die is not when he falls and bruises his side, but when slight stains start appearing on tablecloths and upholstery in the apartment he has so beautifully furnished. The time that was unbearable was when Tolstoy kept repeating: Everything was fine."

Ivan Ilyich would have googled his symptoms perpetually.

Maybe he would have written about it, as if the thing that had *got going* in him were a *good subject*.

His hair, which lay limp across his forehead, could not be repaired for any amount of money ($7.00 to $100.00, depending on style and severity).

A fish blooped in the water, freckled, creamy, and something slid up her spine like a bead of mercury. She thought of Ivan Ilyich trying to catch his floating kidney. Of Ivan Ilyich having to think about his gut. I have been *here*; now I'm going *there*. Calling out to his friends playing cards, Animals! *It* staring straight at him from behind the flowers and Gerasim holding up his legs. And what poisoned his last days was the fact that no one would say he was dying. I am dirt and disorder. I'm flying somewhere. . . .

Two sides, ten sides, all sides.

Death has gone, he told himself. It's gone.

The woman, now a Christian, had read her palm long ago at a party. "Your lifeline . . ." she had said, and pointed to the place where it did not end, just went jumping off the heel of her hand. Perhaps it was the thing she now called the "line of story." She turned away from the memory, lifted her hand, and pointed to a cloud so vague it might have belonged to some high hidden cliff of her body. She would not ask her to read it again, now that she had been altered.

"Any preexisting anxiety?" the doctor asked.

"... No," she said very quietly, though in fact she was the kind of child who was scared not only of the fireworks but of the half hour it took to find parking before the fireworks.

"Any other symptoms?" Her voice rolled up over her tongue and stopped at her bottom teeth. How to tell him *I cannot do my work?* He would look at her—in her Looney Tunes shirt, and her cutoffs that she wore because one day she had tried a sort of wrap dress and then looked down at the crosswalk and hee vaguna was out (that's how she found it written down later, *hee vaguna*)—and say, Exactly what is your work? And she would sit up straight as if on her deathbed, and recite, in the voice of authority that still lived somewhere inside her:

"What makes *Pale Horse, Pale Rider* serious, what makes it real, is its counterpoint. If Miranda had simply spoken of herself, the pains in her chest and her head and her heart—it's not even a matter of believing, no one would have cared. If she had said oh, I cannot write my pieces, my hair has decided to grow in the other direction . . . I have lost that fine, easy seat on myself, astride . . . what can that matter to us? A woman's death is not much bigger than her nightly headache, and no one wants to know about those. It is the fact that she is in love, with the war playing out behind her, and the fact that her young man will die. This is what allows us to love her, a woman like that, with everything in her lap, and her choice of horses."

She could explain that they were always weighing writers to see whether they were good. Not good at *writing*. Hilton would write about Katherine Anne Porter, she would explain—as if Hilton were famous to him, as if Hilton had preceded him too—and he would end with the huge emerald Katherine Anne bought for herself once she was truly rich, and the emerald would begin to glow like a gas, backward over everything she had ever done. And all of them did it, they walked into the writer like she was a night, and lay shivering on the ledge there until they were lifted up by the hand of their own discernment, which was sometimes just the fact that they were alive and she was not. But there was a real emerald, and it was what had really happened, that night she was visited by "all she had ever read or had been told or felt or thought about jungles"; the fact that she had almost died, which she said had separated her from other people for a very long time.

But there was still the portrait of Katherine Anne, with her hair shocked white—oh, if only she could describe what had happened to her, instead of what was happening to herself! With someone else, I can believe everything, and spend ten pages on the twitch of an eyebrow; I can lie on the ledge and be visited by everything I have ever read or been told or felt or thought, until my own hand plucks me up, into the night and the fireworks. She swung her legs sidesaddle, in case hee vaguna was out. THAT is my work, she cried to the doctor!

"Oh no," she thought, as she had thought when the Georgian photographer took her picture in the public park, "am I going to have sex with him?" Because she no longer knew when people had sex with each other, and the neurologist was telling her to *push hard with her foot against the palm of his hand*. "I'm concerned about the weakness in your legs," he said sternly, behind his mask. Was that when people had sex with each other? Was it when they wanted to order an MRI of both your brain *and* your neck? She had been waiting so long to see him, maybe that was when people had sex with each other. Now he was talking about her "jumpy reflexes." "Some people's reflexes are just like that," he said. "My own reflexes are what you might call *brisk*." Uh, was it just her imagination, or was he saying that their reflexes were in love? "Push," the neurologist told her. She had forgotten to wear socks that morning, which introduced bareness into the situation. He had the most beautiful hands she had ever seen, which must have spoken, somewhere back, of a failure to become a surgeon. His name was Ryon, so she could tell people, "He makes me laugh!" "I want to watch you walk," he said, a sentence she had heard a hundred times before. It's not like it could have changed meaning in the night. It's not like you could wake up meaning something completely different, not next to the neurologist, who was telling you *as hard as you can*.

Kissing was no longer paradise, but was rather a place called Eel Hill. This was a hill her mother had encountered when she was a girl, on a camping trip in the southern woods of Canada. One morning she had set out for the lake, with a lunch pail and a towel over one arm, and just before she reached it there rose in her sight a dune swarming with hundreds—her mother said thousands—of independently wriggling yet seemingly connected eels. Go back, her father told her in a low warning voice, as if the eels might turn to her in a single body, smacking two of its longest specimens for lips, and descend.

They were going to find out about her, she knew. They were going to find out there was no sex in her books, despite her reputation. Writing "*getting trichinosis from that little pig wilbur—in other words, eating him raw*" was not sex, which was between people.

Her friend texted about doing it with her boyfriend Lucas, except she kept remembering him as *Lemuel*, so that at one point she nearly asked "how *Lemuel* was hung." Normally she would not have asked such a question. But a man named Lemuel sounded like he would be hung apocalyptically.

Write something sensual, she commanded herself, and after half an hour managed to produce the sentence: *There were few compensations about the new life they were all leading, but daily headlines about coronavirus "lingering in the penis" were one.*

"How many living cats do you have?" the man at the antique store asked her. "Three," she flirted, placing one elbow on the counter, "and the ashes of a dead one on the mantelpiece."

One night she was traveling down, down, through a million sheets of paper, to the center of the earth. She did not even know anyone else was alive. Something was bent around her neck, which might have been part of another person. The chain of her necklace snapped; it had been a gift from her husband. But it happened to be New Year's Eve, and just as she started to come a firework went off, and bells rang, and then the whole world was screaming and frenching itself, and they were rolling off the bed and laughing uncontrollably, because what you were doing at midnight you were supposed to be doing all year long. The cheering went on much longer than seemed possible. Something like her necklace slid in and out of all her holes. She stood naked at the top of the year, which was a mountain. It slithered with minutes. It was Eel Hill.

A special commemorative Alzheimer's edition of *Time* magazine (what were these things? who required them, and what were their uses?) led to a legendary fight known as Just Let People Have Alzheimer's. "What the hell is that?" her husband said in the checkout aisle at Target, glaring at the exploding brain on the cover. "Just let people have Alzheimer's."

Big mistake. She had a proprietary feeling about Alzheimer's now, ever since the new studies had come out. "WHAT?" she yelled, the greatest word in the English language. "Say it again to my face?" "I said," he repeated, "let people. Have Alzheimer's."

"No research! No cure!" she said, making "genius hands" at him. *"Just let people have Alzheimer's!"*

She reached out to touch the brain. She had studied these commemorative editions at great length, though lately the covers had begun to look strange. There was Marilyn Monroe, a deconstructed seashell, and Babe Ruth, a big dirty potato, and Elvis, whose stopped swollen heart was a rhinestone. There was the moon landing, looking as faked as ever, and 9/11, WILL THERE EVER BE ANOTHER YOU? And now this, for if *Time* magazine didn't remember Alzheimer's, who would?

She would sneak back and buy it, she decided, as the argument rolled with the cart into the parking lot, where the usual flock of ominous crows had settled on the tree above their car. When he was in the bathroom brushing his teeth she would arrange the magazine carefully on his pillow, with the exploding brain face up for him to kiss. She had done that once before, with some picture of a woman he especially loved—blue eyes, short ashen hair, somehow tragic—Julie Andrews in clown makeup, maybe?

"The names go first," she told him. "You might happen upon a birthday party in the park, and someone might hand you a glass of champagne, and only after drinking it—you don't drink—do you realize that you know everyone, you've been friends with them for years."

The first woman who ever had Alzheimer's, she read to him from her phone, "'started to become inattentive with housework, purposely hid objects, and lost her capacity to cook. She also developed insomnia, which caused her to drag sheets outside the house and scream for hours in the middle of the night.' Sound familiar?" she asked, and held up a picture of a confused German woman in a nightgown. "Look a little bit like your wife?"

Nearly all of their fights were fake, and this one was no different. Vaguely she thought they were sending up the concept of marriage itself. When they were first married they got only three channels and all they ever played were shows like *My Husband Raymond Is a Problem* and *Till Death Do Us Part (with the UPS Man?!)*. The husbands and wives were locked in a room together, just as they had been—stealing each other's apocalypse bidets, eating the single jar of peanut butter that the other had Prepped. What the husbands did was forget birthdays. What the wives did was try to get a new refrigerator. Yet their faces were stamped in some very soft part of her. They would outlast other things. If she ever saw the raymond or the UPS man in the street, she would stop dead, as if she had spent a whole lifetime with them once.

They passed a car with a bumper sticker that read HONK IF YOU MISS PRINCESS DIANA. Her husband laid long and respectfully on the horn. "But wouldn't you feel bad if I got Alzheimer's?" she asked. And her husband, driven to desperation, cried out, "NO! JUST LET PEOPLE HAVE ALZHEIMER'S!" "I wouldn't be sad," he insisted. "You had lived a good long life." She interrogated the tense: *I had?* "But what if I had to be introduced to you every morning, and lift up my little hands to your face to see who you were, and kiss you for the very first time?" And here she stopped entirely, for that was exactly what he had always wanted—no names, no history, just that glow on the pillow—and why not let him have it? Just let him have it.

Over the past year she had posed in her own window, framed by ivy and wearing a shirt she had found five minutes ago in the laundry basket; under stone arches, wearing a sweater that—she realized later—made her look exactly like the Cookie Monster; outside in the frigid air for hours, her hands folded on a dead stump. Often, when she returned home from these shoots and looked in the mirror, she saw that she had a small surrealist mustache.

Maybe she could look like herself for this woman, who wanted to photograph her between two worlds. "In terms of location, the Photographer was wondering if we could avoid the squares, which will have people passing through and are commonly photographed. She would love to meet you in the parking lot of the Publix; she's interested in the parking lot as an unconventional setting; a sort of built-up liminal space."

"Actually, I'm in the Papa Murphy's parking lot," the Photographer said when they called her. "*It's even better over here*," as if she had crossed to the other side.

"I then experience a micro-version of death (of parenthesis): I am truly becoming a specter. The Photographer knows this very well, and himself fears (if only for commercial reasons) this death in which his gesture will embalm me . . . they take me outdoors (more 'alive' than indoors), put me in front of a staircase because a group of children is playing behind me, they notice a bench and immediately (what a windfall!) make me sit down on it. As if the (terrified) Photographer must exert himself to the utmost to keep the Photograph from becoming Death."

"It would be easy to be dead if I were French," she thought, not for the first time. Barthes had a particular kind of parenthesis (inside it, you are safe from being hit by a laundry van). At that point a man veered in a huge vehicle toward her, stepped out, and then approached with a pen and a copy of her book for her to sign; he had recognized her from the road. It was now her job to assure the Photographer that this had never happened before. But the Photographer was looking at her so weirdly, for so long, that she thought with relief that she could actually do it, she could photograph her as she was.

That day she and her husband had been married for nineteen years, which she knew because he told her. Now he stood in the parking lot of the Papa Murphy's as she wall-sat under the image of a sweating Pepsi. "Get in the picture," the Photographer told him, and she thought yes, of course, if she could not look like herself, at least she could look like *them*. He knelt in front of her with his head resting on her breastbone and she was surprised to feel his thighs shaking against her; despite his strength, he could hardly hold the pose either. So it was as difficult to persist in loving the replaced person as it was to be replaced.

"You remind me of Eras," the Photographer said, as they walked out of the barn where she had been posing on an abandoned toilet. The toilet, sculptural, standing alone in a man-made dusk, had awakened her imagination; with the Photographer's encouragement she had straddled it, pretended to flush it, posed for a John Singer Sargent portrait on it, with her dress slashed deep down the middle of her chest and her face nailed up in a shaft of light. The light is what they kept talking about: Is it going? Do we have it? Is it gone? When she drew back the corner of her skirt to reveal the toilet the Photographer had shouted YES!, as if it were the most secret part of her body, never glimpsed before by anyone but the man standing in the background. On the toilet it had come back to her for a moment what a human being looked like: dawdling, self-regarding, solitary, pushing back the half-moon of the hour with the tip of her orange stick. *You remind me of Eras*. She almost cried. What a good thing to say to a person outside time.

The Photographer herself was barefaced, and looked like a dry paintbrush. After it was over, the toilet, John Singer Sargent, the Eras, as they walked back through the liminal parking lot of the Publix, she confessed to reading Craigslist Missed Connections at a time of great loneliness in her life. What if someone had seen her, across a crowded room? And thought, *Her* I must meet. That's the one, as the photographers always said when they finally got the shot.

Someone, she did not know who, had signed her up for the Word of the Day. "Eustasy?" she asked, the first time she opened the email. The illustrative picture was of a navy blue wave networked with foam. The ad, which showed the grim revolving dance of a skeleton's hip bone, was

"5 Bone-Dissolving Foods Seniors Must Avoid." She was almost tempted to click. Maybe that desire was what had put her on the list.

Every morning at nine fifteen punctually, it arrived. And went through phases, like the moon. For a while it only gave her words a body could be preserved in, like *peat* or *quag*. Then it gave her words for the body itself—Pia, *the delicate innermost membrane enveloping the brain and spinal cord*. Then it turned its attention to the sphere of ideas: prescient, eureka, immanent. Who was doing this to her? It felt targeted. But still she waited for the drop in her mailbox, learned the new word and its attendants faithfully, and finally felt herself called on to choose. She went around in the world as the Word of the Day, weighing, considering, rejecting. One quality of diarrhea is *intense meteorism*, she read. She did not have diarrhea. But she had the comet inside her that made her write that down.

A sickness in your synonyms, she knew, was the beginning of the end. In word-finding tests, they told you to name farm animals, or things that were red, but she was after something broader and more fine. She flipped to the end of the notebook and in a very secret handwriting wrote:

> *Patch acre region domain plot mile farm square garden field rectangle triangle circle site yard hill dune shore bubble cove hive island peninsula apartment nook spot dimension plane hemisphere house palace oasis glade stretch zone orbit chamber*

The list grew stranger and stranger—alp, she wrote, and nutshell, and wineglass, and envelope, and chapel, and shoebox, and Ireland.

When she finished that, there were others to be done: Sounds, Colors, Pulses, Integuments; she would rebuild it all from scratch, she thought, not just her language but the entire thing; Appendages, she wrote; Plasmas, Pangs, Durations, but always returned to the original list, which grew till it covered the world, every corner. Pocket, she wrote, and felt a great hand pat her. Quag, she could write as the last word on the list. Page, she thought, and saw what it was: *Places a poet could put you.*

If the whole element of air could suddenly be sucked into a whirlpool, and then begin to lift up the sea and the carpet of the land, then this could happen. If it could be made to rain, hail, if even houses could, for a moment, serve tea in the middle of the sky, then this could happen. And our familiars be lost, be stranded by flooding, and come home a year later with the bells on their collars ringing. Hadn't the brindled bulldog done that, after Pa left him to ford the swollen river? If this could happen in books—a whole family crawling across the floor in their nightgowns, begging for dippers of water.

They were leaving that place, that was the sick body. Let me on the roof please, she had begged her husband then. There was a door at the back of the bedroom that they never opened, that would only allow you to walk through it once. Let the air in, she gasped, but there was no air. Smoke detector downstairs going off night after night at three a.m.; the nurse below them near death or on meth, motionless on his couch and blasting EDM. He must have thought it was part of the music; it was. The alarm never stopped and they forever smelled smoke but nothing further ever happened. She and her husband taking turns to wonder what were those fireworks going off in the closet, just at the very corner of the eye. Did you see them? Did you see them too?

Come closer, please, I have it. Certain things could only be recognized when they were described in the body of another person, like that lady in *The New York Times* who had become paranoid about the color red. Paranoid about the color red? What would that even entail? Yet in that place she was afraid of her own floors, how was that possible? The brain—trained to leap, only to discover its accustomed landing pads were gone. Midair, it repeated the words falling, falling, falling; a step out the door was a step into orbit. Everything so fast. Pattern rode over the earth like a horsehide, rippling sometimes under iridescent flies. Light through the leaves. Tail switching. She could only control the flying, the rushing through the universe feeling, if she imagined herself on its back in a printed dress, long braids that she had never had streaming out behind her. The rough texture of a pencil drawing, and feet as slim as trout. Strange snippets singing in her mind. At first she could not place them, and then she remembered: There was a found poem she had been writing called "Manifestations of the World's Aliveness in the Works of Laura Ingalls Wilder." It was the culmination of long years of highlighting, for the books were full of sentences that would never be found elsewhere—a phosphorescent signature that no one else seemed to see. Nibblings of fish and devourings of grasshoppers, jerkings down into deep water, rippings of the ragdoll, leeches stretching away from your legs: the landscape taking small bites of you, to incorporate you into its own flesh. Most of all she wrote strangely of horses, riding them endlessly into the horizon—or as if the earth itself were one, and its last two lines running up the reins and into your arms.

Up the warm, slippery, moving mass of pony.
She and the pony were going too fast
but they were going like music,
nothing could happen,

face was one big shining of joy,
nothing could happen to her until . . .

The music stopped.

Her doll was still her doll.
The light shone through them.
There seemed to be voices in it.
Rode right into the sun as it was going down.
Go on in the sun around the world.

Three weeks after they moved to the new house on the islands, a wind came in a pillar from over the marsh, attended by patches of rainbow and feldspar lights, and deposited a shower of tiny iridescent shrimps around the pool. And why be surprised? she wondered, surfacing from a long, lung-bursting dive that seemed to separate the old self from the new, with the light net of glitter on her skin that meant she was soon to catch something, some meaning. It had happened where things happened before, in the Bible.

Her friends splashed and idled around her, talking about the lab leak theory. The words had lately begun to sound mysterious and wonderful—she imagined a beaker shattering somewhere on the other side of the world and the contents making their slow crystal trek toward her address. "What's the closest you ever came to being a conspiracy theorist?" she asked her friend Maryann. For her, of course, it had been that the pope was not the real pope, and then, taking it a step further, that none of the popes had ever been the real pope. Her husband suspicioned dark things about microwaves, that canned foods were "putting their cans in him," and that Rivers Cuomo had been secretly replaced after a car accident in 1996. Her little sister, addicted to the History Channel, seemed truly to believe that an alien had been Jesus, or the other way around.

Maryann lowered her heart-shaped sunglasses against the glare, like a normal-aged Lolita. "I once told a guy I was dating that I saw how the moon landing could have been faked."

"My friend Chris the Canadian was a moon landing truther," her husband immediately joined in. This was one of his store of high school legends, along with the friend who had been born with his dead twin in one ball and the rest of his organs on the outside of his body.

"*Not that I thought it was*," she clarified, raising the sunglasses again, "just that I saw how it could have been."

The composite that was poured around the pool was a pale porous beige and made of crushed shells. Curled up in its craters, each shrimp was smaller than an eyelash, a wish, and the color of angel skin coral. Not dead, she decided, in stasis, dazed. They would wake and find themselves as she had: on the surface of the moon, at the house on the islands, as new as Rivers Cuomo, as unreal as the pope. "I'm the only one who's noticing these SHRIMPS?" she said in a sitcom voice, but was frightened; if you were the only one who could see a plague, maybe it was directed at you.

"The Eleventh Plague," they agreed, skipping over the one that had just happened. "What were the others?" "Well, there was sleep, and there were crickets, and a pig blotted out the sun, I think," her husband said. They looked it up. Boils. Flies. Hail and fire. Pox. Maryann had been with them on the last normal night—watching *Titanic*, screaming TURN THE WHEEL—but hadn't gotten sick, it had skipped over her house. A swipe of blood. Something about children? A darkness that could be *felt*.

We are the plague, people had said at the beginning, rejoicing over pictures of empty streets, of fish and animals shyly returning to natural habitats—and the farther removed she was from the world, the more she felt it was true, that *Nature was healing*. Every so often it went around about the plague of frogs, how scholars couldn't decide whether it was a lot of frogs or one big one. One big one seemed kinder, the size of the sky. "Drop the whole shrimp on me at once," she said to the Lord then. Death? Her whole life? The big book? All the days?

They had bred the sunflowers to look horrible. "No," her husband corrected, handing her the bouquet and rummaging for a vase, "they bred the sunflowers to look the way Van Gogh saw them."

Recently she had started pronouncing it Van Gah, she had no idea why. Van Gah, Van Gah—if she wasn't careful, she would let it slip now. She peered inside the whispering cone of green paper. "You can't breed a flower to look the way someone sees it."

"On the contrary," he said, "that's *all* that you can do." This was delivered with satisfaction. He had an eye, which meant a wide field in which images grew. When he took her author photo, he gave her directions like *Look alive* and *Do something else with your face*. Last time she had cried when he said *Look alive*, so then he changed it up and shouted, *You're a new grandma!* and that was the shot they had used, the one people would see long after.

The sunflowers really were a nightmare. They had been removed from their hot dry field in Provence, from the free untrammeled growth of Vincent's eye. The last time she looked at one of his pieces, she had seen such tremendous pathways in the paint—even the short strokes seemed to beckon her over some hill; she looked away, she was in danger of disappearing, pitching away like the haystacks, turning gold with the doorknob and stepping into that bedroom. . . . "In the nineties," she said, "we called him Vincent, and we thought he was our friend, and we were always trying to figure out exactly what kind of epilepsy or schizophrenia he had, which is not something a friend does, really."

Her husband shook his head. He actually had epilepsy. "And we would make a movie about his life where Counting Crows did the soundtrack, and the actor had to wear a bandage around his ear the whole time. And the soundtrack would be going"—here his voice slid—"OHHHHHH VINCENT."

"That kind of ruled, though," she said, which is how all these conversations ended. An age, whatever else you might say about it, really did kind of rule.

They had visited Provence two years before, and the thing was that it actually did look like that. "Monet was a plagiarist," she had realized, walking past the glassy run of his lilies in the wild—she had assumed he had invented them, but there they were on the outside, trailing ribbons of blue and lilac and green. And what was the thing we had believed about Monet? "That he was a frog," her husband had said; only a frog would know some of the things about lily pads that he knew. He looked untroubled at the landscape. He refused to make art himself, he said it was for crazy people. A book, especially, tried to force you to see things—tried to breed you, in short, like a sunflower. The field in his eye grew imperceptibly; he clipped three wayward grasses from it. There. Better. Good.

But here were Van Gogh's sunflowers. Horrible. Individual hairs like the nape of a human neck. Standing up, always, at whatever sight or sound. What is a flower's ear, she wondered, pulling off three of the petals and feeling the tug in her own flesh. "The best thing," her husband said, "is that they just don't die, not like the regular ones."

"How did they do it?" she asked over her shoulder, *How did they make them this way?*, but he had already moved on. He had found the flowers and brought them home, the rest was for the artists. Through the open window came his Counting Crows falsetto, perfect, which only she would ever hear. Every morning for the next two weeks, he would say the same words, wide enough to include her: Those things are lasting forever.

"Have been attacked by a Rottweiler and am in the ER," her father texted from Kansas City, when her mother and sister had been visiting the house on the islands for two days. "Do not panic."

She thought she understood. There was a cusp in the air; they could all feel it. For the last six months, craftily, in secret, her sister had been inventing the vaccine. Had even given herself two doses while pregnant, to demonstrate that it was safe. Her father would refuse to take it, of course, believing it put barcodes in people. But she would welcome a barcode, to keep track of herself—a chip to identify her, lost and shivering. "When Mary glided through the door, on that gold track that now carries people to me, and wrapped me in her long freckled arms," she wrote in the notebook, "she burst into sobs but could not let go fully, as she could *had I still been her sister.*"

Maybe "attacked" was not the word. Their brother Daniel, who had been a witness, said it looked more like he had walked into a rosebush. But her father had insisted, had even called an ambulance for himself. (Her brother: "Yeah, when the ambulance guy got there, he was like, 'Why did you call an ambulance?'") Her father believed the dog had been trained by its owner to hate the Catholic Church. It had been sicced on him as Christ's earthly representative. He had a hematoma the size of a grapefruit—he was a great believer in things wrong with the human body being exactly as large as fruits—but couldn't send a picture of it, he claimed, because there were no cell phones allowed in the waiting room. The surgeon carefully debrided the wound *in case there were any dog teeth left in there*, his words. Oh, it was typical,

typical! Whenever her mother was gone more than two days her father died of a Popsicle deficiency and called her back to identify his body in the morgue. After she hung up, they had all gone into fits of laughter, and she thought, that is the lesson: You must live your life in such a way that your children do not laugh when you claim to have been attacked by an anti-papist Rottweiler.

Her father's main sign of decline over the past few years was that he kept increasing the number of stories about dogs he had killed. The number had gone up to *five*. No one knew why he was doing it, because he loved dogs more than people, but there you were—in the hospital room where she sat gently tracing the lines on her niece's hand, her father was telling the story of having to extrajudicially execute a German shepherd to a woman who kept repeating in the regional accent, "Ah, wow." He seemed to think it was party conversation.

"What if dogs *did* hate Catholics?" her husband said. "What if when the altar boy rang that little bell, all the dogs in the world burst into the church at the same time, barking?"

"They eat up the hosts..."

"They drink from the baptismal font..."

It was her turn to say the best one, "They fetch the Cross," but she was thinking of something else. "Remember when Dad got the idea to breed puppies?" she asked, but this venture had ended so badly that she and her sister put their heads down on the table and almost cried.

"Wait, what happened to the puppies?" her husband asked.

They had all been born with holes in their hearts. They were so unfit to live that she wondered if she weren't one of them. There was a pen in the basement, lined with the classified ads, and pictures of her father cradling them in his T-shirt. . . . Maybe she was the one he had held at his breast, and maybe she was the one going after him now. Maybe the reason she didn't want to see him was that he would know right away—she wasn't herself, she was a Rottweiler who had been trained to go after the black sweep of his robes. If she ever burst into his house again, and padded softly up the stairs as she used to do, never calling out "Dad" so as to surprise him, and eased open the door to his room where he sat alone in his underpants, she knew what she would see: the gun pointed at her, the hole in the heart, the number of stories about dogs he had killed gone up another notch.

Her father claimed to be pressing charges (against the dog?). He claimed to be appearing in court one morning, for this attack on his person could not stand. Searching through the records, her husband said there was no such case.

"I dreamed he went at night to a place called Banjo Town," her sister said, rubbing her eyes, emerging from the guest bedroom in the morning. Shanties in the woods along Devil's Backbone, a dip and a curve across the way from their grandmother's house. Thumping floors, music pouring all night long, and they couldn't find their little brother Daniel, he had gone ahead of them there.

Immediately she could see it, through gaps between trees. Past the butcher, over the crest that dropped your stomach, behind that bar that was actually called the Holy Grail—and she hadn't heard the first part, that it was a dream, so she went into the place where her sister was having it, in the mazes and recesses of the skull, like a fish darting into coral or a candle bobbing through a cave. The flare of the match that lights up a human face. Could you do that, enter the personal labyrinth, with someone who was *that* close?

She poured coffee, as if to sober them up. In the cave you passed others, prone or motionless, who had gone there or were trying to get back. Following the thread of voices and clashed glass, the center of the earth cracked open to ice. Who would you meet in the night? Not yourself. Who would they meet in your shoes? Someone new. And then you were among tin chimneys, jugs of moonshine—the mind had a front porch too, where you went to talk and never know what you were saying.

Normal people don't dance that way, her husband said on her twenty-first birthday, dragging her off the dance floor. But being dragged was funny to her, as was the fact that she had had twenty-one shots and something called a Sex with Alligators, and she wrenched herself from his grasp and ran back to grind. You stop speaking *English*, her husband used to tell her. You disappear for hours looking for a guy named Weezer. You end up in a holding cell under Paul Brown Stadium, soaking wet. It happens to all of you. But what a relief, not to speak English. It was unzipping the body and stepping out. It was knocking the sharp corners off everything in the world. Certain rooms of drunkenness—whatever happened in them kept happening. Her crawling across the dirty floor of a diner, making friends with a dog.

Had it begun with the long purple scars down her brother's neck, that call from her father, *Don't worry, I saved his life?* Hey baby, she had whispered to Daniel from the doorway, after her red-eye flight back home, Hey baby. It was like going to meet him for the first time—some unknown scent in the hospital room, compressed, dark, spilled—and realizing, as the nurse puts him into your arms, that he smells like the inside of your mother. And looks like you.

They let them take him from the hospital to the hotel, all of the siblings crammed in the backseat like they were children. Things snapped back to what they were. Even in that extremity, their mother disappeared every morning—a bottle episode, Heidi had proposed, *about where your mother goes*—and returned four hours later laden with bags from Trader Joe's. They shopped for soft clothes for him, for where he was going. He had called her that night to ask for help, to restore him to reality; she had been sleeping. It was her father who knelt over him, stopped the bleeding. *My jacket was talking to me. It told me to break the glass. . . .* When she thought of what had almost happened her heart felt like a stone in her chest, that the pure flesh of the peach had pulled away from. It beat and she thought, how far away. Why hadn't she been awake, to pick up that call? Less tipsy that night than usual, knowing something was wrong. Her husband rousing just enough to draw her down toward him, to murmur from his pillow, He'll be fine.

Before bed her sister put on a pink robe and rubbed oil into her stomach so she wouldn't get stretch marks. Her daughter, a totally new kind of person, was in her belly; "I just felt she was protecting all of us." The room as closed as if they were walled up there, the red scent, the whole family together. She had gone before her brother into this life, she should have done more to guide him, left drawings and diagrams on the inside of their mother. But here he was ahead of her, escaping, leading her out of the woods behind the Holy Grail.

People lived their own lives, that was the thing that surprised her. They had nothing to do but live their own lives. It wasn't like pomegranates, where the first pomegranate she ever saw was the first pomegranate he ever saw too—the same memory of their mother bustling in with her bags and saying, "Look what I brought home from the store." And then all of them breaking it open together, and painting the whole kitchen red; stained, their father stealing the seeds, all of them entered into the same dream.

There were the rooms where it kept happening, clustered together, makeshift. The city you had built, out of what you had done and what had been done to you. Heart-long thumping, silken liquid, a river somewhere speaking. The whole place filled up amber to the very lip. This is how the story moved. This is how things happened to you. When would the day come, when you wouldn't have to do it anymore?

Maybe that was the beginning, of the knowledge that things did not end. Three years later, he was safe in the world with them, he had left it, though at night they still saw it, indelible images, the firelight flickering. I dreamed he went at night to a place called Banjo Town. And their mother, coming into the room just then, cried out, I've *seen* those shanties!

The woman in the next room was scromiting. She sounded like a gorilla, or the guy from Disturbed. The whole hospital sat in the palm of her hand, rocking back and forth to her experimental music. RUAHHH, the woman went, in long waterfalls, but only when the doctor was in the room.

She was in the ER because she couldn't feel herself going to the bathroom. Everything was suddenly very difficult: lifting her left arm, raising her left leg. She felt that she was trying to sing one of the Emily Dickinson poems that couldn't be sung to the theme song of *Gilligan's Island* to the theme song of *Gilligan's Island*. If you told them that, they thought you were having a stroke and kept you, even though all the beds were full. Maybe they kept you if you mentioned poetry at all.

Any alcohol? they asked, at the end of some dark tunnel, and she told them no, none for three years. Family History? Why yes, she said politely, that was certainly possible. Her brother PJ had gotten it and for a period of twenty-four hours believed he was back in Afghanistan. I got us here, and I will get us out, he told his children. Do not be afraid.

The light hurt, as if she were evil. A dead body was wheeled by under a Navajo blanket. Flat on her back in the bed that had opened, she found herself praying to the Little Flower, who was both a woman and the underfunded grade school she had gone to. Picturing her face, like an endless breadstick, and the habit wrapped around it like a dark brown napkin. The Little Flower will cure me, she thought, though she would have been so happy to have this suffering herself. Pain is simply nearness to the red-hot Him. She began to picture the Little Flower bent over and scromiting, and how joyful—how joyful!—the *scr-* part would have been. And how bountiful the *-omiting*, how unto the Lord.

"RUAHHH," went the woman next door, and she laughed, thinking of the full-throated OOOO-AH-AH-AH-AH she used to do at readings. Always a crowd-pleaser, and really it took a surprising amount of skill. Did the woman practice at home, or just trust that when she got to the hospital she would be able to do it? She rang the call bell for the nurse. "I'm pretty sure I'm about to have to go to the bathroom," she said, but the nurse looked skeptical. The same thing that carried conviction on a stage made her untrusted in here. It was Presence, and Presence had nothing wrong with it. It stood in the middle and spoke, it was *there*. I feel that I am being pulled out of the world by the hair—this isn't the Best American Essays, bitch! "Do you mean that you are dizzy?" the nurse tried to clarify. "Yes," she said after an obedient moment. "Maybe I mean that I am dizzy." But she meant that she was being pulled out of the world by the hair.

Her friend Jamie, an expert on movement, had once told her there was a tiny dance that went on inside her all the time. She had told her other things too—that her husband was not connected to his Pelvis, that she was walking around like she didn't know she had a Tail—but had never mentioned the existence of a DJ who could suddenly start blasting *The Sickness*. The door opened and someone entered; elderly orderly, she thought, elderly orderly. "You got a lil old bra on?" he asked, as he wheeled in the machine to take her chest X-ray. She sat up and tried to perform the old trick—unhook the back, pull the whole thing out through your sleeve—but it was like a bit where a comedian pretends his own hand is trying to kill him. "Excuse me," she kept telling him. "Almost there."

To feel that you are not able to control your own body, as if it is a thing you are writing! To feel you are a marionette hung up at night by the neck! "You feel that you are not able to use your arms?" the doctor asked, when he came in with his clipboard. She attempted a scrupulous, first-confession honesty. She had never confessed to her *father*, of course, but gold Heidi thought, for narrative purposes, that maybe . . . "No, I feel that I'm about to not be able to use them. Are you yelling at me?" she asked the doctor. "No," he said, in a gentler tone, "people have been unable to hear me all day." "So you feel that you are about to not be able to be heard," she said, nodding.

"I think I can go home now," she reassured the doctor. "I mean, I'm not going to die." "No, you're not going to die," the doctor said, laughing. Still, he had to have it on record: that she was acting of her own free will. Why did she wish to leave? "Someone else needs the bed," she told him, someone with monkeypox, maybe. "I am wasting the nurses' time." She could not confess the whole truth: that every time there was a code red, she thought it was a fire drill, and tried to put on her shoes and go outside.

In the car she glowed bright, from something they had given her called the Contrast. Her head was like a vodkamelon rolling backward off her neck. But safe in her own bed, at home, she prayed. Prayed not to be cured but to be a saint again, as she had been at nine years old. Longing for that great burden to bear: the body. The Little Flower, if she was about to not be able to use herself, would cry, "Take me to heaven, O Lord!" The Little Flower, if she were unable to feel her own ass, would know she was already there, on a cloud.

And am I the only one? a woman asked, of the feeling she called the Tickness. It had first happened to her at six years old: She was in bed with a blazing fever, a blanket was laid over her arms and legs and at once the blanket felt *thick*. Then the feeling crept into her throat and arms and legs, thick objects entered her brain, thick furniture, stairs, thick cabinets and carpet, all marched on her and crowded her atoms, and the Tickness as she called it took her over. It was worse when she looked at things like winter jackets, patches of plaster on the ceiling, meringue, but anything could be part of the thickness feeling. It was like being snowed under, or stitched into the quilt, or sucked toe by toe into the tarpit. She had to cancel plans with friends when it happened and simply wait to die. It was geological. It was grass growing over the forms of the dinosaurs, even the ones that flew. All were laid low, were overtaken by the Tickness. She did not speak of an opposite, the Thinness, that borders, skins, windows had all disappeared, that everything had become fine crystal, singing, that the roof was gone and she was released up, and up, past mountaintops and sundogs and the zigzagging angel, toward a hole in the atmosphere just her size.

Deepest conversion on record, her father had claimed, and now she was having the highest. A terrible desire had possessed her: to hold a copy of her childhood Bible. It was a shoebox then and it held dioramas, wherever she opened it, a different one. The Tower of Babel like a solid sandstorm, the burning bush on cellophane fire. She got smaller, she went in and walked around, or else it became large. The costumes looked real, the people made of clothespins, the Popsiclestick cross where jokes shone through red sugar. Whatever was evidence of its construction disappeared or did not matter. It was happening and she was there.

In the valley of dry bones she was rising and rising, trying to remember how the body had been. Open the Song of Songs, and faces were pink with rampant lambs; breasts were heaps of spices, feet turned to burnished brass; the simile was laid next to you under white sheets; and every single *like* came true, from the mouth of the anonymous poet. And the cover looked like her name when she was not expecting to see it: a field all full of little yellow flowers.

And she believed. People stepped down ancient roads and she fell into step alongside them, carrying all her possessions in her hands, one neat square of them no bigger than a . . .

She tiptoed out to buy one, raising puffs of ancient dust. One *Bible*, she planned to say casually, to whoever happened to be working. No, that sounded strange. One *The Bible*, please. She had been avoiding the bookstore because whenever she stepped in, they asked her to sign—but her *T*s refused to be crossed, her *O*s bounced like Oholibah's, and between the first and last was the floor of the parted sea. But now someone was holding out to her a New American Version. A *New American Version*, was that possible for people? It was, it must be, it had her name on it. The whole box and everything it contained had everything to do with her. She lifted the lid and looked inside. Brown leather sandals, size 7½.

"You must not tell him that you wrote that story about him," she told herself firmly, in the examination room at the neurologist's office, "because then they won't let you see him again, and he's the only one who has anything to do with you now." He didn't knock as he entered, which she liked—the room was his. He closed the door and turned off the light and showed her dozens of slides of her brain on his laptop, small and bigger slices so that she seemed to grow, and she laughed out loud; she hadn't known it would be funny. He ignored her. A scene of play and concentration was spread before him: a game of Risk, porn in the woods. If they had let him, he would have looked at the pictures all day, and he spoke with great jealousy of the doctors—surgeons, with even more beautiful hands—who had access to totally dark rooms, dark as skulls, where they sat talking not to the patients but to the brains themselves. He raised the lights and recoiled from her, she thought she could see why. She had, for a brief moment, become interested in it. This was a cardinal sin; you could not become interested in the illness. You could not lavish on it the love and solicitation you had previously lavished on the self, even though it was the thing that the self had been replaced by. You could not, though the brain told you to do it, laugh out loud: that it looked so much like a creature, in a painting of deep time.

That night she went walking for him down the long hall. It opened out, and splashed up her ankles, and flowed into her childhood creek. Hamilton County, she liked to tell people with pride, was one of the richest fossil beds outside of Lyme Regis. But as a child she only knew that you found things there, if you looked sideways and down with soft eyes. The dream was to discover a whole skeleton intact, but that was after the creek's time. It belonged to an age when the whole land had been a waving sea, so what you found were broken-off branches, printed with breathing flowers, or brachiopods like silver nutshells— all of it the same absolute gray, so when the little mermaid sang, you saw her on a seafloor where light filtered down among layers of liquid shale.

It was such a sacred place that even her mother came there sometimes, to play. She never found anything, since she was no longer a girl. But one day they had seen a whole sky full of violently waving clouds—mare's tails? mackerel?—which were so different from anything they had ever laid eyes on that afterward they became a kind of shorthand. *The clouds*, she would say to her mother significantly, and her mother would look her way and nod, thrilled and solemn and circumspect. But one day she made the mistake of uttering this password in front of other people, and her mother pretended she did not understand. *The sky*, she said in the deep undersided voice of meaning, and there was a moment of silence, and the others began to tease her by naming things all around them, and her mother joined in finally and mocked the ground, Tricia, the ground! Afterward she would hear her mother's voice, rocking under her, *the ground!* And in the end she did not even know which one of them had betrayed the other.

Knowing where to look was one thing; knowing where to step was another. There was one slab of bedrock in the creek that held a little bit of everything, swipes of shells and tiny stars and segments of crinoids, all struck to stone at the same moment, like the whole world had lifted its eyes at once and seen the sun through waving water. The Cincinnatian period. Those clouds called undulatus. The slab looked firm, but would lurch when you stepped on it, to remind you that it really all had been ocean once—and who were you to think you were different, that you could be the first to walk on land.

Then there was her Galapagos feeling, a green teetering inside her, splintering of finches, the breathless incipience of a new species. It happened underwater, or in the middle of the air; she had been on the Islands a million years and look what she turned into.

"There's a Galapagos, Ohio?" she heard her husband asking her mother on the phone.

"OH YEAH!" her mother screamed in her OH YEAH voice.

She saw a great swooping in the corner of her eye: Her husband was making the motion that meant *Write this down*. But she shook her head and turned away, for in her mind she had begun to flip through something her mother had received twenty years ago in the mail—a large coffee table book full of glossy color plates, purporting to prove that evolution was not real. So much money had been poured into it that her mother was instantly swayed. What would she have seen, looking at the pictures? Not animals at all, but little mothers and fathers, and babies turning out exactly as you intended. "It's so well produced!" she kept saying, pressing it to her chest like a sixth child.

"No, you know what's well produced?" her old self had answered hotly. "A baby tortoise on the Galapagos Islands, with perfect little . . . fingers!" She still retained some of the rhetoric. Even when she finally managed to escape from that house, the last thing she saw before she got to the airport was the Creation Museum, which featured a full-scale replica of the ark to prove that everything in the world could fit on it, and where the gift shop sold T-shirts reading, "God created and I believe."

A woman had posted a Google review of the Galapagos Islands that read "Almost the perfect getaway, but not sure who snores louder, the Tortoises or my husband?!" This was a review of her husband rather than the Galapagos Islands, but people were always making that mistake. Leave a husband on the Islands for a million years and see what he turned into—an arrow straight from the quiver of the species, talking to her mother on the phone!

"What is she saying?" she mouthed, and he lifted the phone away from his ear, so for a moment her song entered the air. "*Birds are evolv-*

ing to sound more like car alarms" is what she heard, so maybe it was only people she couldn't believe it about. She turned a page in her mind and found her last self, teetering. If she could no longer trust her legs, perhaps another transport would arrive, that would fly and keep flying her past the Creation Museum. Look at her husband, it had *optimized him*. The page went out from under her like the edge of a cliff, something was coming . . . she was going to . . . what did the Google review call it?

the most place ever . . .

Time to look up the Google reviews for Galapagos, Ohio, except there weren't any because the town was actually called Gallipolis. "Gallipolis," she hissed to her husband, "*Not* Galapagos. *Gallipolis.*" And instead of being the home of Charles Darwin, it was the home of Bob Evans. Her mother certainly believed in *him*. She believed every word out of his mouth, which was a menu. Bob Evans was across from her childhood church and she felt she had been born in him on one of the tables. *Family Restaurant*, she had chanted as she walked through the doors. *Family Restaurant*. Every Sunday she waited there in her mother's skirts for their name to be called; her fingers on the fabric were perfect. Leave Bob Evans on the Galapagos Islands for a million years and see what he turned into. A hole full of fresh warm eggs.

But new people still were possible. There was her nephew, who was at this moment sitting on her lap and reaching up toward the ceiling fan, which went around like the world. His cheeks shivered whenever she spoke to him; he had never seen people before. This was interesting. At what other point in history had so many babies never seen people before? Shut up in their houses with their mothers and fathers, shrieking when they saw the strange mailman. Oh, is that what happened to me? she thought. Born again? The purpose of the visit, in part, had been to show her the baby, so that she might recognize him. But when she buried her nose in the top of his head, she smelled nothing; clear, a wisp of cloud, the swirl of her own hair.

"Who's that?" she whispered, touching the baby's nose. The baby's cheeks shivered when she spoke to him; he trembled around a drop of water. She thought her father must have baptized him in secret, in the bathroom or under the kitchen tap, for in the catalog of things he wanted, there was a page of souls. Hers had been one, once, and probably he thought he still had her. "Say _____," she said, reciting her supposed name. Then, whispering, "Say *Dennis*," and looking into her mouth, the baby achieved recognition as a pond does: He rippled and was still. The lost blue eyes were raised to hers. Meaning was suddenly hitched to its star. I got us here, I will get us out, she told him. Do not be afraid.

Part Two

Presence

"Everything you're saying makes perfect sense to me," my friend enunciated slowly, "because I am a dancer."

I could feel the bowl of mascarpone and fruit slipping spoonful by spoonful inside her, plumping each red cell like a raspberry and allowing her to speak. Cycles that had once taken ages were now instantly completed; breath burst the balloons of words; the time lapse of everything bloomed painfully at the limits of my head. This was what I had tried to explain when I said that now, when I witnessed the movement of any living thing, a small body of sensation was created inside me. When I watched the cat washing herself, for instance, something inside me, fur covered, five bones, moved itself in luxury over the ledge of a face.

"I was watching *White Christmas*," I told her, "and my eyes didn't know where to look, couldn't get enough of anything. I stared into their dancing until it seemed I could do it. Vera-Ellen was like a firework, exploding away from her own middle, and when she bent over to drink the malted I felt like I hadn't eaten for a year. I felt like I could move all my furniture into the whites of her eyes. I felt . . ." I stopped, for she was nodding. If I told her that I felt like my blood had been put in capsules and distributed to Halloween stores across the country, she would know what I meant: She was a dancer.

All day we had been talking about Presence, and the Six Viewpoints, and Red-Nose Clown Training. "Clowns are the biggest masochists on earth," my friend said, for to become a person who could elicit anything from anyone, you first had to become a person from whom anything could be elicited. She rolled her eyes, as if to communicate that she had taken enough shit from clowns on this planet. The cat jumped onto the table and arranged herself in such a way that would elicit love; my friend ignored it, because she believed that cats, too, could be enrolled in the school that taught you to act.

In the past, we had had huge screaming fights about Gene Kelly, during which I often executed an incompetent spin move to prove my point: that I was glad God had killed Gene Kelly. But all that was behind us now. We missed, both of us, standing onstage and feeling the self like a thrown voice in the corner of the room. For a year and a half we had not been allowed to do this. My friend had recently taken over a production of *Urinetown* (the original director had been fired for suggesting that gospel music in fact came from Ireland), at which no audience at all had been present and everyone onstage had stood six feet apart. The dancers threw themselves at each other from great distances, and held up stethoscopes to plexiglass panels instead of each other's chests. This was terribly moving; when I pictured it, I felt a pain in what could only be described as my Presence. Life was pulses striding over the huge green heart. Everything that lived was a throb of sensation divided from the next by an arbitrary costume. I had never seen my friend naked, because her whole skin was a leotard—watching her stretch the spoon up and down, I felt bare feet slapping against the boards, and tights hanging up to dry, and a trip we had taken to the Danskin outlet once, where I could still feel in my elbow how I had knocked down a whole rack of trembling pink torsos. And what was I wearing then that could not be stripped off, what was I wearing today?

"Watch this," my friend said, and sent me a video of a real dancer.

The stage was laid with rectangles of rich dark dirt, and she seemed to be making decisions with parts of her body that other dancers had no access to—all the way down to her hemline, all the way to her split ends. She tried to plant her feet forever; it was frightening. Make a small body of sensation out of *that*, my friend was telling me, but I could not feel the dancer, only the nude skirt washing itself like a waterfall, only the worms in the world, only the pencil in my hand in high school as I drew Igor Stravinsky upside down. I raised the hand with the pencil, it was a spoon, I took a bite. The cat turned and swept through the heavy red curtains that hung inside me. She must have known the Six Viewpoints already—space, story, time, emotion, movement, shape—for the fine fur along my back stood up and stirred, all the way to the tip of a tail.

The small body of sensation, when it washes itself, is so soft, so sweet, so unprotected. What do I do with it? I wanted to ask. I am holding it somehow, and it grows heavy in the arms—how do I tell it that's enough now, it's clean? Now my friend was opening her mouth, in the middle of a spotlight on a stage inside her chest; auditions for the self took place every morning at ten. She threw her self to the corner of the room and laughed: The answer was simple. I must enlarge the small body of sensation until it was as big as I was. I must let the paw become my paw and the face become my face and wash one over the other in eternal rehearsal. I must kick out a leg, give up my old life, and become a cast member of *Cats* on Broadway—which had been running now for a hundred years, which would run another hundred more, until at last one night the star was out, and I was the one who was chosen.

The Artist Is Present

Nothing more frightening in all that time than a book arriving in the mail with my name on it. "Read a little from the beginning," someone would ask, and I would open it, my heart going two hundred beats a minute, knowing that soon I was going to hear myself say *Van Gah*. "She opened the portal."

I am supposed to be talking about fiction. Instead, through the screen in the center of my apartment, I am talking about the real. You aren't trying to explain what she means, I say. You are trying to open like a flower the fact that she was there. "Do you want to see a picture of her? Do you want to see a video of her singing?"

It feels like desire, the interviewer says—that must be the reason we find ourselves speechless, weeping, doing an unintentional reenactment of *The Artist Is Present*. She is back in her teenage basement; I am gesturing at her with my new strange hands. It is desire to be in the world together, parallel, silent, showing each other things on our phones.

"It's like Joyce Carol Oates is trying to start a feud with me," I say. "Does everyone have this feeling?"

For three weeks straight I have nightmares about being asked about *cancel culture*. It is my greatest fear, to be asked about *cancel culture*—or that I will be so terrorized by the possibility that I will immediately begin talking about it anyway, and in doing so present the opportunity to be murdered by public opinion myself. Because all my subtle calibrations have been lost. I no longer know what is OK to say. "I am going to be the Aaron Neville of literature"—was that all right?

Her cat is carceral, I imagine someone saying. *Be aware*.

I am readying myself for another interview when the crowd bursts into the Capitol. I have to go get a haircut, with my phone held tensely in my lap under the barber cape, and wonder the whole time whether the Speaker of the House is having her head chopped off. The haircut itself is administered by a stylist in his fifties who believes in me in a way that no one ever has before: that I can carry off an early-nineties Fly Girl situation. When I step out of the salon and back into the stream of what is happening I have a feeling that I have possibly never had before: American.

The purest poster, many were saying of the ex-president, the one who loved posting the most. He had been permabanned and was floating like a spirit looking for a body to possess, eventually attempting to manifest as @garycoby. Gary Coby. So it's nothing to do with me, I realize. Just a fortuitous time to have published a book about the internet being the end of the human mind.

An eighty-five-year-old woman writes the craziest thing about me I've ever read in my life. Good for her, I think.

The first sign of trouble is that you begin to believe you are lying. The second sign of trouble is that you begin to believe you are not a person. The third sign of trouble is that you begin to believe you are bleeding out, through speech, the living images of those you love. Memories that are allowed to run on inside you maintain a kind of vascular velvet, a receptive lushness that stirs with the grass, air in every pore. But what am I thinking about? Maybe if I hadn't written about my niece I wouldn't have anything to hold on to at all. The past year seems to have erased time backward. I text Maryann one morning in a panic. "Did David Bowie die? I dreamed that he did." "Girl," she responds, appalled, delighted, "David Bowie died five years ago."

"So I did predict it then," I say.

I am to be dressed and lit like a "Dutch painting," for a remote photo shoot in my apartment. Coincidentally, it is the same night my sister is to be induced. I maintain the same position for two hours, framed by a window overgrown with ivy. (No photographer, on meeting me, ever wanted me to leap, or even smile. Always the Dutch painting thing.) But, "Is she having the baby?" I keep whispering to my husband, who has one foot almost in the cat box, trying to hold our most flattering lamp over my head. I cannot feel anything from the waist down. Jason feeds me a handful of cashews very carefully, through my motionless Dutch lips. At one point the photographer accidentally deletes all the pictures and we have to start again. "Is the baby being born?" He better hurry, I think, so he can have his picture taken. He better hurry, so we can interview him about his breathtaking debut.

"Did I talk about not being a neurotypical person?" I ask Jason, who listens from the other room in case I need to know something crucial, like where I live. "No," he says, "but you did talk about having synesthesia. You said you saw ice cubes every time you read the word 'refrigerator,' and every time you heard a fife, you thought of the Revolutionary War. I don't think that's synesthesia," he says after a moment. "I think that's just knowing what words mean."

"I see Descartes as a little beaker of water." Who doesn't?

Headache, I would write, though it was never located within—it was more that I joined some headache outside me. "Some days the delirium seems to return. It feels expansive, uncomfortable, as if pathways are trying to break past the outer walls." "Solid objects seem to rain." "My reading comes and goes like a magic store." And: "So strange. Even to touch rough paper is agony. This is why Howard Hughes used to sit in the dark naked, watching *Ice Station Zebra*, his fingernails long and yellow as a record holder's."

"I do not know if she is interested in ethics," the eighty-five-year-old woman said. "I think she is a genius, but I do not know what kind." There are only two kinds, and one of them is: evil. So now I have that to worry about as well.

One woman who interviews me turns out to be a TERF, which I only realize when I get an email from her saying that she *spent all morning online arguing about gender*. That can only mean one thing now. Well wait till she finds out about Dennis. When the article comes out, it features a picture of me sitting cow-eyed on a park bench with the words *Not a neurotypical person* printed underneath, as punishment.

The juxtaposition makes me seem like a case study in a medical journal that has been allowed to choose her own clothes.

"Y'all staying neurotypical?" my brother texts the next morning.

"That moment," the Dutch man says to me, moved, "when you see the baby's tee-tees on the echo." The Dutch, I remember from my visit to Rotterdam, had a kind of woman called a *Patrish*; they would point to someone on the street and cry out *Patrish!*, but I had never been able to find out what it meant, and they had—thank God—never aimed it at me.

During an interview about what I find sexy—TODAY, TOMORROW, and YESTERDAY—I just keep repeating that when I was a child I think I was attracted to Ewoks. Their short stocky bodies. Their leather vests. The bucktoothed decision with which they bit into those little crackers. "I'm not sure what I'll find sexy ten years from now," I say, so stressed that I realize I'm crying.

"That wonderful part, where you meet the Canadian, and his friend hands him a business card that says *I've seen your balls* on it . . . tell us what happens next." "Hahaha," I say weakly. "I do remember that. Yes."

I am asked about the internet, the internet, the internet. "Once, at an anniversary dinner, my husband ordered thirty-six oysters by mistake, and had to eat twenty-four of them by himself. As we were walking home, he grabbed his stomach, turned to me, sloshed, and said, *Twenty-four oysters have become one oyster.* The modern internet," I finish, "is where two dozen oysters go to become one oyster." A pause. This was the point, in person, where I would hear the audience making little yum-yum noises. But now I couldn't tell. Was that anything?

The Polish interviewer, on the phone, "You placed a jar in Tennessee, and round it was, upon a hill. Was that like your feeling for the portal?"

> *The wilderness rose up to it,*
> *And sprawled around, no longer wild.*
> *The jar was round upon the ground*
> *And tall and of a port in air.*
>
> *It took dominion everywhere.*
> *The jar was gray and bare.*
> *It did not give of bird or bush,*
> *Like nothing else in Tennessee.*

I am surprised for once, but yes, it was. "It was like that," I say.

Before we all wise up and get ring lights we appear in dark caverns, like Greek myths. This is better, I think, than the high gloss that comes later. We look like what we are. We look like transmissions that our loved ones will watch over and over again when we die. Before my talk with Bertie I write in an email that before, doing events in other cities, I would always go to a drugstore and buy two lipsticks, one that was the exact same color as all my other lipsticks, and one that was practically black, for some reason. Airport hypercaffeination led me to believe that I could "carry this off." It was like going away for the summer and returning to school to spell your name Jenipher. Out of a sense of nostalgia, I go to the local Walgreens and perform this ritual again. I settle on the black one—unprecedented, as I would always apply it in the brutal light of my hotel bathroom and then immediately wipe it off and put on the color God assigned me at birth: Ohio Mauve. "Are there other things you're going to do when we get back in the world?" I ask Bertie; for myself, I keep thinking about buying sunflowers for my hotel room, sometime in the blue future when I am Jenipher. "Oh, it looks so good," she gasps when I appear on-screen, another reason why I like her. Also because she tells the truth, like about those "horrific shits" you always have to take just before you go onstage.

In the midst of it all, a request from Pamela Anderson to ghostwrite her autobiography. Months in a hotel room with peppermint tea and both of us wearing red swimsuits, the leg holes cut so high we don't even need to speak. Her, unburdened, made lyrical, and me, immersed in another life that involves pencil eyebrows, good calves, and sex with Tommy Lee. I consider it.

You must be there, someone tells me, on the phone. Everyone else will be there. You cannot win if you are not there. So I go, so strict with my mask that I barely eat or drink, and float suspended in the large worldlike skull, which is enlarged by my crisscrossing flight, eight hours across the ocean, a vaccine card and a test that reads NOT DETECTED in my pocket; I have Kafka's journals in my lap, I read over and over the passage about his trip from Milan to Paris—not altogether voluntary, as he said, for at that time they were all outrunning *the cholera*.

"I'm trying," my agent says, reading the first new pages, but she can't quite follow. "It needs something, some detail. Like one time I was on a bus with a dog that I thought was really deformed—like for three hours I'm thinking that this dog is really deformed—and at the end of the trip it unfolded itself and it had just been sitting in a weird way?" She's right, it does need something like that. You unfold yourself after a long journey and nothing is wrong at all. Take me there, I want to go with you.

Ushered into a white tent outside Heathrow to be tested. The young man in a mask so strangely gentle, as if I don't understand something fundamental about what we're doing, reaching the long swab up into my nose to touch my brain. *He'll be telling me to put my mask back on now*, I think, but he doesn't, and just sits looking. Dark hair and long crossed forearms, the mothering, fussing-over-a-chick look of some men. It's like the neurologist or the Georgian photographer, some undressing past undressing—and only me naked, he believes, but my mind fills in his face.

Now, in an alternate version of London, I find someone who is like me. We even look like each other, maybe—I feel our faces slide over each other like ovals as we speak, and time begins to travel forward. We are sitting in a pub that is famous for literary conversations and now we are having one. "I sleep with a stuffed pig," we say simultaneously, and it is famous. "What's your pig called?" Susanna asks, and I shake my head, too shy to tell her that it's just . . . "Mine's just called Pig," Susanna tells me. And writes me afterward, *From Pig to Pig, and love from me to you.*

It happened to her too, after a book tour in America; some virus, she doesn't know where or when. Ten years in a dark room, writing about a man in a maze. Saying she put something in the text of her masterpiece when her brother . . . but she doesn't finish. A pencil point just touches down in my mind. "And let it remain there," she says, "for a long, long time."

Over lunch, I am told of a woman who listens to my life story every night as she falls asleep, and how it is "really causing problems in her relationship with Etienne." I want to meet the woman, but more than that I want to meet Etienne—held in a bed against his will, the voice like a terrible river. Is it my *literary project* to follow Etienne around, leaving little messages in his mailbox? Now she's at lunch, now she's eating miso cod, now the cameraman is threading the microphone up her dress just as she realizes she's wearing insufficient underwear. Updating Etienne on my daily doings until he is forced to take matters into his own hands . . . but then bliss, silence, no description of it, peace, and sleep, sleep, sleep, sleep.

I start my period on the train to Bristol and start crying in the loo and the lav because I can't remember how to use British tampons; freely bleeding, I have to mince out like Gollum and ask my publicist to explain it to me. At this, my mind kicks off a photo reel called *Embarrassed in Front of the British*, which includes an incident where I disparaged Freud in front of a renowned Freud scholar and the man sitting next to me sucked in his breath sharply and laid his fork down next to his toffee pudding with kind of a loud sound. Actually this little sequence always cheers me up, even seems to cure me for a moment. You know that you're alive and might live forever, when you're Embarrassed in Front of the British.

I am struck by the lights on the stage, by the podium that tries to embrace me at the knees, by my feeling of the bodies of the other writers, the swoops their gestures make in the substance between us, which is not air; when one lifts an arm an arm lifts inside me, when one smiles

I am split apart; *I can see their souls*, I think again, they sit in bright curves on the tops of their heads; when they speak a pin pricks my lungs and all the air rushes out; my heart is going two hundred beats a minute; one has no hope and I love him, another has hope like fever and I see myself smoothing his hair; a child of fifteen sent in the question, I myself never utter a word, about whether fiction is justified, about whether we can add white ice back to the world; and I sit in the bright light melting, melting toward Mollie, fifteen, who had asked.

"You had it at the very beginning, didn't you?" the novelist asks me, his face a picture of tan, tender disbelief. "I'm almost envious of that experience, to be one of the very first." A real novelist, I think—again with love, at last. A safe receptacle for the thing in the chest. He will be the one who wins, at our distanced ceremony in the BBC theater, and I will know because a woman will come out with a powder puff beforehand and powder his tall shining forehead only.

"I think if you have access to ten hand signs you can convey the fullness of human experience . . . I think if you can blink out a page with your right eyelid you can convey the fullness of human experience . . . the doctors describe a lack where what you are experiencing is abundance. I think we turn our opposition to the diagnosticians of the age. It is overspill. It is abundance. We do have the language." I scream this, yes, directly into the mouth of the former Archbishop of Canterbury. Impossible to describe the sequence of events that led me here: completely orange, with a chemical burn on my lower lip, dressed as a gothic Lolita and hollering about plenitude. But I have come to welcome anything so strange I will remember it.

"The anniversary of her death," I write. "After I was sick, I never felt like I was visited by her anymore. I only had dreams where she was turning blue while I was watching her, or where she was twisting in pain in my arms, arching as far as she could away from me, tipped backward, by the heaviness of her own head. And in those dreams it was not her but my own body crying out."

I don't just cry when John Lanchester quotes *King Lear*, I cry later when I think about John Lanchester quoting *King Lear*, and later when I tell the story of crying when I thought of John Lanchester quoting *King Lear*. "I cried when I listened to your talk with John Lanchester," a woman tells me. "He quoted *King Lear*."

This is the event I will remember, the first, the only. The light is melting, it's the best part of the day; my whole bra is showing, but I won't know that till later. I'm not sure how it happens, but some distance collapses and it is a real conversation. He talks about George Eliot, the growing of the grass, the roar that lies on the other side of silence. He quotes *King Lear*, "Never, never, never, never, never." He is sipping a glass of white wine and I feel the tannic draw in my own mouth, that physical focus; I haven't drunk at all for years now. "I can't read *Lear* anymore," he says, just Lear, as if standing there in robes were the real one, loved and lost. Why should a dog, a horse—a book—have life, and her no breath at all? I think I was crying; perhaps he was. What is this feeling, across people and cultures, that the dead recede from us not so much in time as in distance? "Never, never, never, never," and we said the last *never* together. To be in a real room again, all of us, breathing beneficent air.

Hashish in Marseilles

"I got your child," my older sister Christina had a habit of saying to me. "I don't know how it happened, but I got your child." By this she meant that her firstborn daughter remained in the unconscious body, not shaping her gestures to human sight. Sighght. Wasn't that some kind of poem? Angel was as tall as I was now, and had glasses and a rope of red-gold hair that she wore over her right shoulder. Very often she chose not to speak, but retreated into a kind of peacekeeping within herself; had the self-sufficiency of an island, which grew breadfruits and shelter and shade. Had a private language full of pleased loanwords, from films and television shows and other people. Needed nothing and needed everything. Wanted to be a writer. So had I been.

She had been homeschooled, like the other nine children (no, eight, but I kept saying one too many), and I was giving her weekly classes, which was very funny, considering. Literature .001. Mostly this meant we would read a few pages of whatever I was reading and talk about it. We had started with *Romeo and Juliet*, but since Shakespeare was one of my more notable degenerations—"Oh look, a Hobbit," I often said now, when I saw a Shakespearean actor on film—I developed the sly maneuver of asking, "What's this about?" and waiting for her to actually tell me.

Today, insanely, we were doing Walter Benjamin's "Hashish in Marseilles."

"Go ahead and read," I told her, and sat back with relief to listen. "First I ordered a dozen oysters. The man wanted me to order the next course at the same time. I named some local dish. He came back with the news that none was left. I then pointed to a place in the menu in the vicinity of this dish, and was on the point of ordering each item, one after another, but then the name of the one above it caught my attention, and so on, until I finally reached the top of the list. This was not just from greed, however, but from an extreme politeness toward the dishes that I did not wish to offend by a refusal. In short, I came to a stop at a pâté de Lyon. Lion paste, I thought with a witty smile. . . ."

Lion paste! That must be why I had chosen it. I waited for Angel's smile, and it came. I started to laugh and she started to laugh; many things in the human being are contagious. "Connections become difficult to perceive, owing to the frequent sudden rupture of all memory of past events, thought is not formed into words, the situation can become so compulsively hilarious that the hashish eater for minutes on end is capable of nothing except laughing. . . ."

I could not tell her what had actually happened the last time I smoked weed, after an event at a Boston bookstore. I took the tiniest puff, tried to stand up, and fainted dead away. "No, you didn't faint," Jason contradicted, "you just sat down very softly on the floor and whispered *Hospital*. You lay there motionless for a long time, convinced you were showing everyone your vagina." Vaguna. "Then you crawled on all fours to the podium and drank an entire pitcher of cucumber water."

It was true, I had never handled drugs well. Nevertheless, I had embarked on a hallucinogenic program to heal my mind. A friend had sent me a matched pair of mushrooms in the mail and, being in the mood to flout the law, had included a mushroom stamp with the words *ha ha* written next to it. The mushrooms were tiny, woody, perfect, and looked like the child of something. All right, let the cure begin. I would drop two dark gills of them into my opal cup, pour hot water over, wait, and then, as the hooks and eyes of things began to sharpen, open a coffee table book called *Baby Wetland Birds*. This featured extreme close-ups of, you guessed it, various wetland birds as babies. The chapters were all called things like "Ducks and Goslings: The Little Dears!" My husband often found me, after drinking the tea, staring at the book with tears running down my face. I felt like a chick covered with oil, dying, and a tall woman was washing me with liquid detergent. "I will never forget a fucking feather of these baby wetland birds," I breathed. The other things that had happened so far were that I had (1) become 10 percent more psychic and accurately predicted the death of several musicians, and (2) developed an insatiable hunger for chicken paprikash, which suddenly I was able to make.

The blue notebook had been filled, and I had bought a new one: a mushroom diary. "I feel incredible," I wrote in huge curly script, not mine. "*It's mushrooms*. Do you know how good Bunny Wailer sounds when you're on mushrooms?" The blessed state would only last about forty-eight hours, but for that duration, time once more went in sequence, words marched in their sentences, and people on the beach walked in and out of the songs. It was my old feeling, I thought, of flowing out of the pen. "You're playing that good good music," a man called out to me at Fisherman's Walk, and I made the *eheherrherr* sound that I now made when strangers spoke to me, a little closer to real language this time, and scampered ranchously down to the lip of the water.

Also I had invented the word *ranchously*. Incredible that someone had been able to write beautifully, philosophically, even *ranchously* about this experience. The cat sauntered hugely into frame, her beard flared like the sun's corona—she loved to be on-screen, for she understood that she was famous. In her infancy she had been such a notable physical disaster that she was given the name MITTENZ KITTENZ by the local humane society and then almost flung at us for free. We had to sign a paper saying we wouldn't sue them if she blew up or anything. She was *that* unprecedented, that one-of-a-kind. Recently she had eaten a psychotropic skink and seen God, and now a rumor was going around the internet that she was dead, like a Beatle. Now that trip diary would be worth something, I thought—possibly more than mine, which had slid off the rails with no warning into a weird close reading of the Russians. Her eyes had gone black and she had shit like a human being and then lost control of her back legs and collapsed, cawing like a rook. Oh my God, I screamed, she's blind, thinks she's a bird, she's dying! I couldn't bear to lose her, she was my daughter. But she couldn't get enough of this feeling, apparently. The experience had flung open her doors of perception, and the second she was able to stand again she had scrambled into the sunroom to try to get another skink.

Back to the business at hand: broadening horizons. "Have you ever felt sorry for a dish you didn't order?" I asked Angel. "Or shame at the thought of sitting at a table too large for you? Have you ever stood outside a brothel, marveling at your lack of desire? What does this sentence mean to you: *The more closely you look at a word the more distantly it looks back?*"

She shook her head, puzzled, still in the unconscious body. Part of the project was to give her an understanding of metaphorical language—I would show her that Sighght poem, and a light might switch on. "I was always feeling high as a child," I told her, to encourage reminiscing; her favorite assignment so far had been to write her own version of Joe Brainard's *I Remember*, which I had read to her with all the hand job parts removed. "I would have a Coca-Cola Classic (I always called them Coca-Cola Classics, because I thought otherwise people wouldn't know what I was talking about) and exit my body. At Buzz coffee shop, after my second refill, I would ask my friends, 'Do you ever feel like your hand *is coming out of itself?*'" They would look back at me in amazement—all of them lesbians, some of them drug dealers—and say the same thing always: Are you high?

Something like that was always happening, even in books. I would catch my breath because a few lines ahead, I would see a word that reminded me of "forest." Not the word *forest* itself, but like a light bobbing into it, and then I was following into the forest too, and the fragrance and the *thought of what might happen there* was like a knife-edge pressed to my belly. No one else I ever spoke to read this way, except maybe my mother, and in her the tendency was so strong that she never read at all. Maybe she couldn't read, we joked. Many of our confusions were the same, either passed down or innate. One time we had had a panicked conversation: Which two colors mixed to make blue? Yellow and green, we finally agreed, though we went about uneasy for the rest of our day.

I saw a bright blue tail disappearing into the cat's mouth. Christ, another skink. In her throes last time she had hurled all over the mad notebook, which spelled disaster for my archives; almost touchingly, I persisted in thinking that someone might want these. "Freeze it!" my preservationist friend barked, near hysteria. "Freeze it for forty-eight hours! Then, taking a little horsehair brush, sweep gently from the center of the page to the edge." She drew a deep breath and tried to calm down. "Now tell me one thing: *Is there puke on the text?*" But perhaps it was most accurate to leave it, I thought. Then anyone who read it in the future would know how it was: rents in reality, colors falling on colors, cries like a baby from nowhere. A little wisdom rose to me: There is always some puke on the text. Heartening, too, to realize there were other custodians. That anyone could care about paper so much, even beyond what was written on it.

My niece, without knowing it, imitated the rises and falls of my voice. In a fragment called "Child reading," Benjamin wrote: "His breath is part of the air of the events narrated, and all the participants breathe with his life." I passed her the text and waited for her to come under its influence. Some parts of the sentences swelled like hands, others turned to show gargoyle faces. "Do you know what hashish is?" I asked her. "Have you ever been given something that made you feel weird—cough syrup, Benadryl, laughing gas?" My niece confessed that once she had been given ear medicine. I slammed my fist down on the desk. "Write, then, of wandering through a city at night on your Ear Medicine!" I commanded wildly. Everything suddenly become intimate and strange, feeling sorry for too-large tables and the things you cannot eat, the words on the signs looking distantly back at you!

"So what does this teach us?" I asked, and waited. "That under the influence of hashish," she told me, "Walter is truly free!"

Circle of life, I thought, to hear someone you had cradled as a baby casually refer to him as *Walter*. He was trying to tell me something, from his seething port city on the edge of the sea: that we were alive there, all of us. He had written of the aura that makes a work of art itself. I was trying to prevent something from happening to me, to her—that thing that MITTENZ KITTENZ was safe from, in her splendor—our duplication in an age of mechanical reproduction.

But Angel streamed beyond me, long hair from the head of history. She herself was fully emancipated. She had turned nineteen years old on the nineteenth—what she called her *golden birthday*—and to celebrate had gotten her ears pierced. "That's what it is," I could have told her, the moment of difference again and again; the stutter of flesh, the glowing gold stud, sighght. Write about it, I would tell her at the end of class, so you remember everything later. Describe your surroundings, so that we know where we are. Are we hot, cold, hungry; what are we carrying on our backs. Who are we, and wait for her to actually tell me: *enraptured prose-beings in the highest power.*

Mr. Tolstoy, You're Driving Me Mad

a mushroom diary

At the beginning of each little chapter you walk through a doorway. There is the detail of a coffee cup, a mirror, a pear. You must raise the hand to hold, the face to look, the mouth to drink. You supply the blood to the text, the fullness is the fullness of our own flesh. This is why the heart beats with Anna Karenina.

This might be the definition of a domestic novel, one that is entered through such doorways. But we have decided, for various reasons, that this one takes place on the world stage.

I tried to read it when I was young, perhaps even the Maude translation. It was my mother's high school copy, the color of tallow or bone, with Anna in profile on the cover wearing a ring of pearls. And I saw something when I read the word *ball*, which must have had to do with Cinderella. It descended from the ceiling, and was round like a pumpkin, and it opened. And it lowered and lowered until everyone was inside it, dancing in that clockwise whirl of skirts that I felt around my ankles. The shape of the skirts echoed the shape of the word. White necks rose into conversations. What they were saying did not matter much; the real excitement was being at the ball. Entrances and exits, and snow, and Progress, and the horizontal shape of what was coming.

I was thinking of Korsunsky, the master of ceremonies, saying that "he and his wife are like white wolves, everyone knows us." And I posted "a dj who travels through time . . . trying to find the job that is closest to being a dj in every historical era." A DJ would say that now—"I am like a white wolf, everyone knows me." A *very* white wolf. Shout-out to his family!

But everyone just kept answering, "Bard." A few poor people said, "wouldn't he just be a musician?" Jason: "So 16,000 people know about djs, and fifteen guys are like *what?*"

A Mormon in Utah, cry-laughing, said, "What if he were a cantor in a church?" And this is what brings us back, I said to Jason, to the Jean Kendall theory of personhood: that no novel can contain even our own mother-in-law, that we are aliens walking among each other, each in a separate bubble of universe, laughing at the joke however it comes to us. This is how Anna Karenina reaches us, as we are.

"Anna read and understood, but it was unpleasant to read, that is to say, to follow the reflection of other people's lives. She was too eager to live herself. When she read how the heroine of the novel nursed a sick man, she wanted to move about the sick-room with noiseless footsteps; when she read of a member of Parliament making a speech, she wished to make that speech; when she read how Lady Mary rode to hounds, teased the bride, and astonished everybody by her boldness—she wanted to do it herself. But there was nothing to be done, so she forced herself to read, while her little hand toyed with the smooth paper-knife."

The instrument of her destruction is not the train. It is her body, slice, slice, moving us from page to page. The satanic quality of Anna is her need to move, to and fro in the earth and up and down in it. Not to read but to be alive, her eyes so open in the dark she herself can see their brightness.

Vronsky considering the black trousers that contain Anna's husband's legs.

How far did I get the first time? I remember Levin gave me trouble, and his farm and his articles and his brother Nicholas's musings on capital. But I remember those little brown rooms too; I must have tried to move through them. And understand! The surplus value . . . of labor? And the word *ruble*. A cube of cool raw potato in the mouth.

"Karenin was being confronted with life—with the possibility of his wife's loving someone else, and this seemed stupid and incomprehensible to him, because it was life itself."

Mushrooms, I wrote in the notebook, and the headache lifted, the whole feeling of discontinuity, and I could even sit in the sun. I could even listen to music. And the outside world entered the music, the trees were swaying and waving their arms at the concert, and the banana leaves were playing keyboards, and a skink ran into a song and rested there.

I consulted *The Rarest of the Rare* for more information. It told of a man named Schultes who traveled down to Mexico in 1938 to find those mushrooms that the Aztecs had used in their religious rituals. He wrote a scientific article about them that caught the interest of the vice president of J.P. Morgan; the banker also went searching, and published an essay in *Life* about his experiences with those little mushrooms called "the flesh of the gods."

Quite a paragraph: "A group of pigs received a psychoactive dose of psilocybin, while a separate group of twelve pigs received inert saline injections. Half of the pigs were euthanized one day after the administration of psilocybin, while the rest were euthanized one week later."

And: "Psilocybin reduces marble-burying behavior in mice." RIP to those mice, but I'm different.

Anna Karenina. This idea, in reference to Sviyazhsky, of the reception rooms of the mind. What if there were a person whose mind had no reception rooms, but who carried you immediately into the tabernacle?

When his love is answered Levin becomes like the crystal you set on a newspaper to magnify it, and what leaps toward him is the knowledge that other people love him. The process of asking and answering is what makes the whole language transparent.

My skin was running races. This meant that I was looking at art, reading literature, listening to music; or that I was in the ocean, with a wave breaking just at my waist. It meant that I was reading the scene in *Anna Karenina* where Karenin pulls Vronsky's hands away from his face so that the shame can run out of him and rejoin the natural blushes of the world: sunrise, sunset, fruit, flowers. No shame, no shame, I said to myself, pink peaches.

What if Karenin had breastfed the baby? Karenin should have breastfed the baby.

But Karenin can only be a saint in a world with no other people. His sainthood even requires the removal of the one he forgives.

Karenin believes that his coat has been stolen from him. He turns it inside out and finds it full of violets. These are forgiveness. He believes they are something for him to hold and keep holding, when forgiveness must mean to keep reaching, inside the sleeves and the pockets and the shape of the thing we are certain is gone. This is the turning of the cheek. This is the seventy times seven. Keep searching and you will keep finding flowers, and your job is to give them away.

The wedding chapter—trouble with the rings is what marries you, giardia caught at Del Taco, guests slipping on black ice in the parking lot, the lateness of your mother because she is busy sewing a bra into your sister's dress. This is the human slipping a bit of gold on your finger, standing up to shout, I object! and then sitting down again, having decided instead to bless you. Yet it is not anywhere near as moving as Anna glittering with fever, telling Karenin to put his hands to Vronsky's face, telling Karenin that if he looks inside his coat he will find violets.

"The word *talent*, which they understood to mean an innate and almost physical capacity, independent of mind and heart, and which was their term for everything an artist lives through, occurred very often in their conversation, since they required it as a name for something which they did not at all understand, but about which they wanted to talk."

The Mikhailov chapters are very funny. "It is, that you have made him a man-God, and not a God-man." "One cannot forbid a man's making a big wax doll and kissing it."

Tolstoy—the selfishness of the holy feeling, how it is people that stop us from pouring out our generosity upon them. Inside us our feelings are perfect, as people were perfect in the garden. How good we could be on an empty earth! Hence: utopianism, vows of chastity, the handing over of the diary containing all our sins, because the scrubbing of the soul is paramount. My father did this to my mother, apparently, after his conversion. And what am I, she cried, chopped liver?

But the soul is a floor. It is there to bear us up and keep us standing, not merely to be clean.

Strange how in *Anna Karenina* it is the women who draw these feelings out of the men, but the men who are saints.

Holiness is not about feelings. It is about considering how the other body is lying under the blanket. And perhaps it does require that period of rehearsal. Kitty's playacting in Soden becomes real. She actually has learned how to take care of the dying.

That religion that Karenin takes up, under the oversight of Countess Ivanovna, is his attempt to hold on to that feeling, to grasp something tightly in his human hand. But that is where you hold money. It is not where the real thing is felt. The real thing is that the son believes in his mother. That he does not believe in death, especially not her death.

"He was nine years old and quite a child, but he knew his soul, it was dear to him, and he guarded it as the eyelid guards the eye, and never let anyone enter his heart without the key of love."

"When the candle had been taken away he heard and felt his mother. She stood above him and caressed him with a loving look. But then windmills appeared, and a knife, and all became confused, and he fell asleep."

And what do they want Seryozha to learn? "That the word *suddenly* was an *attribute of the manner of action*."

Anna restlessly moving her paper-knife in the book she cannot read on the train, Seryozha notching the edge of the table with his—both of them refusing to learn the prosaic lesson, the water that is expected to turn mill wheels working somewhere else in them.

Are Anna and Vronsky children? Is their sin the sin of children? Born of an impulse that in another garden would be good?

But the real thing is not in grammar either, nor in the proper arrangement of words—not in making you imagine a coat full of violets, or repeat to yourself the words *pink peaches*, though you'll never get me to believe that, and I'll do it to the end of my days.

Is Vronsky a child, with the broken back of his horse slithering under him, the horse whose body is described in such fine marketplace detail because Anna's cannot be?

Sometimes the detail through which we enter is not material but spiritual, and the room is not the room at all, but a being. I am thinking of us briefly landing on the bare foot of the peasant, and the imprint in the dust "with its five toes." I am thinking of those brief paragraphs on the marsh when we go into the consciousness of a dog, Laska, with her mind full of *they they they* and *where*, and the master coming toward her with his "familiar face but ever terrible eyes," because until she tightens her circle down to that pupillary point she does not know what he wants, what he would have her do.

Always it is social custom and even language that leads us astray. Anna alone is direct as a ray, she is pure emotion, rising into the fullness of her shoulders, her neck, the curls of her hair. Her hands are her action, reduced to restless movement because they have no span. And the child of her love, the "dark-browed, dark-haired, rosy little girl, with her firm ruddy little body covered with gooseflesh" is described as a little animal too.

> The One You Wanted to Be Is the One You Are
> —*Jean Valentine*

> *She saying, You don't have to do anything,*
> *you don't even have to be, you Only who are,*
> *you nobody from nowhere,*
> *without one sin or one good quality,*
> *without one book, without one word,*
>
> *without even a comb, you!*
> *The one you wanted to be*

is the one you are. Come play . . .
And he saying,
Look at me!
I don't know how . . .

Their breath like a tree's breath. Their silence
like a deer's silence. Tolstoy
wrote about this: all misunderstanding.

But it is not just misunderstanding. Tolstoy's people have the little raised hairs. They are as responsive to the fickle currents in human interactions as actual people are. The mushroom-hunting chapter, the dashing of Varenka's hopes, is a master class in this. These currents come from nowhere. They come from the world. They are supernatural, they ripple backward from the future.

Those rooms where Levin encounters the bewildering shape of Society, now wearing white tails and a waistcoat, now a ball gown. Sometimes it is at the opera, sometimes shaking out a newspaper, always fanning out its opinions, which are actually laws. But to Anna it is a real body, and everywhere, everywhere. It may even speak in the smooth, dual voice of the master of ceremonies, who calls the dance: "My wife and I are like white wolves, everyone knows us." Not just in those claustrophobic rooms where Levin must bow to it, but pressing against her as the crush in the station, running alongside the train.

Levin, after he had eaten and drunk well, "feeling that as he went his arms swung with unusual regularity and ease." And he leaves the club "swinging his arms in a peculiar way."

Tipsy Levin's encounter with Anna's soul, which first emerges from her portrait toward him and then steps forward in the figure of a real woman. To Levin especially it speaks, that directness of a ray.

"In their ceasing to live they saw poetry."

Anna: "My writings are something like those little baskets and carvings made in prisons."

Where is the detail that first allows us to enter the body of Anna Karenina? For we are not just inside the actual tempo of experience, which so struck Nabokov that he began scribbling out train timetables, but inside her body as it moves. It is her bust where he has centered her life, as a sculptor would; we never see her feet or legs as we do twinkling Kitty's at the ice rink, in her skating costume so short and tight that Nabokov had to draw it. It is also where he centers the involuntary exercise of her strength; that ray that pours toward any man she meets, and that they experience as seduction, also pours toward us. The portrait of her steps out of its frame.

In the scene of Kitty's childbed Tolstoy abdicates this sense of metronomic time and allows Levin to live several days at once: one trapped inside the horror of his bursting heart and body; one on the eternal plane of love with Kitty, staring into her flushed face and holding her hand; and one with God.

Take off my earrings, Kitty cries, they are in the way.

Levin, of his son: "It was the consciousness of another vulnerable region."

In these situations of extremity people do become the thing called saints, because they give up their rational minds and allow their bodies to do what they know how to do.

Why didn't the Beatles ever write a Tolstoy song—"Thank You, Mr. Tolstoy," "Mr. Tolstoy, You're Driving Me Mad," etc. The first lyric could be, "Anna Karenina, you're a fat one."

My husband, singing:

> *Anna Karenina*
> *You're a fat one*
> *You're overflowing*
> *Your*
> *Dress and it's making me warm*
> *(Pause)*
> *Making me warm*
> *MA-king me WARM*
> *(Pause)*
> *This is*
> *The last train*
> *I'll ever get on*

Tye Munn, sitting next to us at the sushi counter, was telling about his shaman. It sounds so funny when you say that, he said. My shaman. It *is* funny. He said he spent the first twenty-four hours of his trip throwing up white stuff. The next morning, though, "I forgave not just myself, but all mankind."

It is so alive that you still feel that the course could be changed, when we are in that sleepy room with the charlatan Frenchman. But then there is that deadness that enters into the closing chapters, which might as easily be called inexorability. It is because her death has been foreordained, by the news item that jumped to Tolstoy's eye. The composition is now a matter of transport; we ourselves are in the train that will take Anna under its wheels. The sign of the cross she makes before she jumps is not alive, it is only from life. It is the detail of the candle that allows us to enter her, and see the whole scene by the last of its light: Anna dropping to her hands and knees before us, when previously she has not made an ungraceful movement for seven hundred pages, and disappearing under the velocity that has joined her time to ours. And who is there to forgive her? The next chapter opens two months later; we have rapidly passed on.

There can be none of that surprise that was present in those earlier scenes of extremity: Anna ordering her husband to forgive her lover—to release her lover's shame—on her first and incomplete deathbed.

Vronsky now, when looking at the smooth movement of the wheels over the rails, will always see her face.

Anna fastened her meaning on Vronsky; Levin fastens his meaning on the land. "In this way he lived, not knowing or seeing any possibility of knowing what he was or why he lived in the world, and he suffered so much from that ignorance that he was afraid he might commit suicide, while at the same time he was firmly cutting his own particular definite path through life."

We have received your opposition to the railroads, Tolstoy. We will return to the land and keep bees.

We must live for something incomprehensible. Karenin is wrong, doing his little taxes for God; Anna is wrong, building her hospital. Lydia Ivanovna was so wrong she was evil. But Kitty is right, considering how a man's body is lying under a blanket.

To be right is to do what our bodies know how to do anyway, and not ask why. "Take off my earrings. . . ."

Tolstoy must have felt that he was full of love, and that his love somehow curdled when it hit the air. He must have felt that words exchanged in conversation almost always go wrong. But words delivered in a tract, say, seven hundred pages—and no one can interrupt! No one in the world is your wife, and everyone is the girl as she was when she first encountered you.

"He was glad of this opportunity to be alone and recover from reality, which had so lowered his spiritual condition."

The holiness that he felt really was a sort of concentration, which perceived as its enemy anyone who might break it. But this also is an attempt to hold on to the violets; you must give your concentration away so it can return to you. And no I cannot do that either, it is impossible!

Indulge me for a moment in believing that characters really breathe. The choosing of Vronsky is Anna's human impulse, but it is Tolstoy who decides that she will die. It is Levin who chooses Kitty, and it is Tolstoy who chooses Jesus Christ. We are more like Laska than we are even like Seryozha, with our noses at every moment catching the wind, and our consciousness at every moment full of They They They.

"But I can't go," thought the holy dog. "Where should I go to? From here I scent them, but if I go forward, I shall not know what I am doing, nor where they are, nor who they are." For the master, with his terrible eyes, is always leading her to the edge of her own precipice and then telling her to leap, to trust him.

one asked about my father I thought of that stone, which it was possible to hold in a certain way.

I reached again into the aumônière and pulled out Waves in the World. One morning, after my last cup of mushroom tea, I had risen, walked toward my shadow boxes, and named every last one of the stones in a fugue—not of my own volition, it was like the words were waiting. They told me what they were called and what they meant, and I scooped them into the soft linen bag still smelling of century-old French candlewax. An aumônière was where a little saint in the countryside would keep her two cents for the collection, before going on to meet her apparition in its grotto. It is like levitating, I told the woman, being held up to the light, when she asked what it was like for me to think through other people, so intensely that you almost became them. Perfect happiness, I said, swallowing hard, and it had been—homework for the rest of my life.

For a moment I was in danger of telling her everything: fear of my floors, the Refrains, how I knew I was separating from the common run because I no longer believed that Meryl Streep could act. Heat rose into my face. Oh, it was unbearable that there was someone so prevalent on the stage of the world, so prone to playing us, that we knew the way a curl would cling to her neck in humid weather. She was carrying a chicken to the table, she was getting married for the second time, she was squinting into the angle of the sun, she was a pink bubble from the mouth that said the words, she was heavily pregnant, like a peach, with another Meryl Streep—would you mind having a blonde play you? gold Heidi would ask, and gradually the whole family had grown golden hair. The woman had described to me the essay she was writing, which seemed to be about pain: of new people, of the long line of others coming to replace you, love-hatred of baby-faced freshmen. Well, what else was I experiencing? Then I could feel myself almost inside her, backed against a red wall with her heart heaving against mine—oh, she was doing it, she was thinking through me, into hair and eyes and head, into the bend of my elbow at the turn of the stair.

Into my dress for the dance, and standing on my father's shoes. How do you know those things? I wanted to ask, but I had told her, I had told everyone. She had my own girlish haircut. Her name was the one we were using for the mother in the show: Mary. The father must be Gary, then, for Heidi had believed as a child that the names of married people had to rhyme. But the name Betty, for me, was harder to apply. "You . . . I mean, Betty," Heidi would correct herself, every time. It helped to have an actor in mind as you were writing. It freed you. The one we imagined was a pure ponytail, an endless font of reaction: She would give you a different take every time, whereas in my brief foray into the art I thought it was the peak of professionalism to deliver the line the exact same way every night, so none of the other actors got surprised. It was always clear, reading a script, which role they would assign to me; I got the sluts and I got the little glass animal collectors, I thought, fingering my systematized stones; they saw something about me I couldn't see about myself. But perhaps I could be free now, in the figure of the blonde.

What if she wasn't a writer, I had said to Heidi once, desperate to be released from the tarot pack of my own past, which could only be laid out in so many ways. What if she does what you do: transmutes experience into performance? A sort of Spalding Gray, wading out to sea with stones while monologuing. An empty stage with a glass of water on it, on something like a bedside table. Nearly every night now I had an actor's dreams—backstage, realizing I didn't know the part, that I was never given the script or received the wrong sides. Or worse, that I knew the lines but had no ideas. The ideas in acting were so different from what the woman and I did: The whole key might be that you wore a pair of glasses, or used crutches, or chewed gum, and the idea would descend like radiance and warm the cool clay of the character to life. You never knew what was going to release you into the body that was ready: to trust the other actors, to trust the self to truly respond. *Check out my dwarf pouch baby*, Heidi had written, and I felt a little of the old levitation: for the first time, something I would actually say. We had written the scene with the father lounging on the leather couch, idly strumming an electric guitar. We had written the old student—not reappearing, but her fear rising every time she saw a white car. We wrote, "I think my mother was a little in love with him," but how could that be true? Well, I could ask the woman, who seemed to want to be something more, who was telling me she wished that things had gone differently, that she had seen me one daisy-faced morning in class.

Upstairs something terrible was happening to the blonde. I slipped the Scar back inside the pouch and took out the Wheatfield, which seemed to have real wind in it, rippling ripe heads. Deep inside was the Mother, and the Fingerprint, which stood for the child, but there was no Father anywhere—that was back with the long-lost fluorite, that claimed to open the third eye. And I did see it, me standing with my father for once alone, and him shy and baffled, not knowing quite what to do, relying on me to provide the proper sense of occasion. Which waited, as I trusted in meaning to wait. In England, I would learn much later, outside the stones of any school, there was a great standing vein of it called Blue John, which was dug out, cured in the air for a year, and then given to a daughter on her graduation day.

Schutzenfest

That was one way of telling I was still myself: I always saw a priest in the airport. Sometimes two. Often a young one and an old one, appearing to hold hands—though that couldn't be true, could it? Always I had the urge to approach, point at some article of clothing, and ask if it had come from the Almy catalog. Or glance at a pair of socks and say, "Gold Toe, I presume?" "Encyclical," I would sometimes whisper as I passed, to watch the password fly through flesh, to see a familiar face in sudden comprehension change.

Lately I had felt the air full of silver nosedives; pilots were forgetting how to fly. "Be careful," I had gasped to my father, lips blue, when it was happening, but he laughed and said he would never catch it—*he wasn't a world traveler* like me. That was before it was possible for people not to believe in it at all, before it was possible to convert to a perfect atheism of it. In that brief window when the powers that be had made Masses illegal, he had gone on saying them—for himself, he explained. That would be his testimony in court—I said them for myself, and I left the doors open.

What is your relationship to religion now, an interviewer had recently asked me. I had maintained a perfect silence for three weeks, and then wrote back, "My relationship to religion now is that I always look for a priest in the airport, and when I see one I say *priest* in kind of a loud voice." This sounded like a joke but in fact it was a cry: Nothing could resume until I saw my priest in the airport. All flights in the world were grounded until he turned the corner toward me, rolling the trim black suitcase that contained the Mass and holding hands with his younger self.

How was he still alive? The things that had been wrong with him lately did not even seem real . . . floating toe, for one. But there he was, walking across the lawn toward me, wearing his bloodstained shoes from when he knelt over my brother—though it was true that I now sometimes saw colors over things that weren't there. Purple blotches over people's faces, a violent prismatic hole in the center of my vision, a zigzag in the corner of my eye that I referred to as *the angel*. There was, I was convinced at the time, no name for this, and why should there be? There was a time on earth when things were created. There was a time when they were new.

"Hey," he said, holding his hands out in his classic dispensing-of-the-loaves-and-fishes way. Does anyone teach you how to say the Mass, I had asked a bishop once. Is there, like, a dance class to show you what to do? No, he said solemnly, *they just throw you in there*. The bishop was Irish, shy, embarrassed. He knew he was meant to be a priest because he never wanted to go to parties. But the gestures had been born in my father. They seemed to be an extension of his physical surety—which I had taken such pleasure in describing in the pitch. Rocked back on his heels, like the world loved him.

"You didn't call me on my birthday," he said, and I started to explain, but he cut me off. "Like my new bod?"

He looked as different as I must have. He had lost eighty pounds, and a column now ran down the middle of his throat. This was made more poignant by the fact that he was, for unknown reasons, wearing a deep-sea fishing shirt. He claimed to have never had it, though he had never allowed himself to be tested—his fake doctor, who also didn't believe in it, had given him a recent diagnosis of Spots on his lungs, but rather than attributing it to either the new illness or the sarcoidosis that plagued so many former submariners, had told him he was probably just allergic to the rare black-market African wood (bought from an actual van down by the river) that he had been using to make guitars. Amazing sentence, I thought to myself, as all of the sentences about my father were.

Put it in the show, I thought, but who could ever, ever play him? Kurt Russell, of all people, was interested, but he wanted us to fly out to California to reassure him we weren't making fun of the character, and at this point in time that was impossible. Instead, I had been encouraged to write him a letter. "Some of my earliest memories are of watching you stride across desert landscapes while my father, his attention divided equally between your pecs and your rifle, commented that you were one of the *last real men alive*." It was the sort of letter that ensured you would never hear from someone again, that they would walk the long way around your house forever. But that would be for the best, I thought. How terrible to be condemned to live life twice, to look on everything as Material.

"Hey. I've been saying Masses for you."

It occurred to me that those must have been the Masses that were so illegal. When the doors were flung open, so that anyone could walk in, even me.

"Her father belonged to a Cold War Reenactors Club, and one day, during their annual meeting, he insisted on falling to the ground in his sailor suit and reenacting his conversion experience on a nuclear submarine—the one he always likes to call *the deepest conversion on record.*"

That was the new beginning of the show, I had told Heidi last month; it had come to me while listening to my binaural beats app, which made grandiose claims to sculpt your brain waves. "It will explain everything about me," I said, meaning, as I always did now, the Character.

"Wait, did this actually happen?" Heidi asked. "No, of course not," I told her, truthful. But from my current vantage point, I might look back at my life and say that none of it had.

We had played around with all sorts of openings: flashbacks, montages, the Character being born as a puppet through a surreal plastic tunnel, a confessional scene where she spilled her backstory all over a sexy priest, who later turned out to be in costume for Halloween. All embarrassing, all insufficient. But this would do it. A meeting of the local chapter of the Cold War Reenactors Club. It could take place in the same church basement where Alcoholics Anonymous had three meetings a day, with doughnuts and cold coffee. A projector would be playing *The Exorcist* on a screen at the front of the room, the members would be wearing their sailor uniforms, and then the camera would find the face of my father just as he fell shaking to the floor.

"Picture it," I had said to Heidi, just as she often said, *Here's the bad version.* An establishing shot like the ultrasound of a whale, and then the camera traveling through black chambers toward him, toward the devil, toward God, toward me. The light of the movie, the light on my father's face; around him, the glow of big red buttons—all of these, calling out the light from inside him, were the radiations that had produced me. "I saw it," I said, the way I sometimes saw things now, glittering tableaux in deep tombs.

"Where was I conceived?" I had asked my mother, when we were in the research phase. "After he returned from the Holy Land, your father took me up to the lake . . . well, not a lake, more of a mudhole really." *More of a mudhole really.* This is what came to mind now whenever I heard the words "genetic predisposition" or . . . what had the doctor called it?

Family History. My brothers and sisters had all been conceived on holidays, with fireworks and toasts of champagne, but for me it was the mudhole and the Holy Land, where my father had spent six months on a biblical archaeological dig, and where, my mother further confided, he had tried to buy her a long white robe of the kind the women wore there. He had paid and never received it, thank God—what if he had made her put it on? What if she had been wearing it *you-know-when?* The biblical archaeological dig was the same one he tried to send me on the summer my friends went to France, but easier and cheaper to have sent me to the mudhole, where I could have started at the very heart and scooped until I found myself: there.

It had rained overnight, and my father's red shoes were sinking into the lawn. "Where are we going?" I had kept wondering in the car, as we passed the dressed-up concrete geese of the West Side, the pleas for kidney donation, the signs reading PRAY FOR AMERICA, but all anyone would tell me was *Schutzenfest*. A baseball diamond. A frightening civic building, where you might go to cast your first wrongheaded vote. A dark curve of wood behind the bouncy house, and more people, it seemed, than I had ever seen in my life. Everyone's here, my father called over his shoulder, his deep-sea fishing shirt seeming to glitter. Everyone else on dry land, but my father and I walked on water. We were not at Schutzenfest, wherever that was, but in the deep dark middle of the sea.

I hated him, of course. I also hated my friends—or to be more accurate, I didn't know who they were. For the first time in my life I had an Enemies List, which included entries as disparate as "God" and "Gene Kelly." I had added my mother to it—had actually refused to speak to her for two months—when she had foolishly confessed to visiting a Cracker Barrel on a road trip. *How could she*, I thought, picturing her among the old-fashioned candy, picturing her length of life as a lemon drop to be sucked. That's my favorite candy, I thought with hatred, as if it were parked in my own cheek, and she was trying to deprive me of its last moments of sweetness.

And what was the thing my father was always saying now? That he was *addicted to reality*. How alive he must have felt, saying those illegal Masses, how made for the moment. Not an object of derision, I explained to Kurt Russell, for who was laughing? I heard the sound, but could say it safely, certainly not me.

The ground was littered with tickets. There was the unmistakable feeling of a raffle going on, and my number being chosen again and again. "What are you working on?" people kept asking me. Little stories, I would evade, and leave it at that, because if to write about being ill was self-indulgent, what followed was that the most self-indulgent thing of all was to *be ill*. But I was determined to do it. I was going to write a masterpiece about being confused.

There was a faint hope that this year could be skipped with no loss of essential information, like a rap skit. Don't write about it, people warned each other, but I had been documenting in secret the whole time. "It was happening in Ohio," I wrote, "even in Ohio." Last November, before the vaccine, my brother PJ had sent a text:

> Last three boomer-as-fuck posts that my
> buddy's uncle posted before dying lol

The first, reposted from "Mary and Jesus," was an underwater statue of Christ with the words "You will get miracle in next 1 hour" printed below. The next read "Before you cancel Thanksgiving and Christmas with your loved ones, remember that this may be the last holiday you have. We are not guaranteed a single minute on this earth. Stop living in fear and embrace life to its fullest!" The last was an X-ray of a rib cage with an image of Jesus photoshopped over the sternum. "Do you see Jesus Christ?" the post asked, with a huge green arrow pointing to him. "IF YOU SEE JESUS TYPE AMEN and SHAR."

That's one of the symptoms, I told him. You get it and it makes your posts weird for one year. Also it makes your pubes as soft as a chinchilla. I had posted about that myself, in the aftermath, and was asked to write about it for a women's magazine.

"I . . . kind of love it," Heidi had said, about the Cold War Reenactors Club. There was something fresh about her voice and something tossed-back about her hair, as if she had just raised her head from the water fountain. "My body has been *good* to me," I could still hear her saying, from the last time we had seen each other, in the heart of the frozen city. Heidi wrote plays because she heard voices. *I say uh I say uh.* But her dialogue was not broken; she poured out long flexible sentences, rising and falling, in the voice that even I could recognize was a treasure. *Hazelnuts,* she had declared in a voiceover once, *they're getting more popular.* When you were writing with someone you tried on their words to see whether you might say them. I put myself inside Heidi's broader shoulders, the tossed-back hair, the dancer's posture, the belly that had then held the twins.

I had watched her, off-Broadway, tell the story of her life, as all the Clintons sat in the same row as me, and Bill got up to piss at the most serious moment even though no one else was allowed. *How did you do that?* I asked afterward, but she had no idea—when it came to the things you were actually able to do, you could never tell anyone. A gift, like being the only one in the theater who got to piss. When I made her read my part, it meant that I was getting it for free. Her voice came over the phone, swimming through that square of darkness; I built her every moment. Reconstituted her, as they might do in the future, not from our frozen brains but our ideas. The hair thrown back. The water fountain.

My body has been *good* to me.

I had chosen her because I had a dream about us drifting out to sea on an ice floe. I understood that might not have been an omen of success, to float out to sea on an ice floe. But there we were, together. Rented houses in the Hollywood Hills, rented houses in Brooklyn, rented houses on Tybee Island. The sun slowly going down on each other's faces. Me telling her everything that had ever happened to me, in case it might be useful. "What is this story about?" the development team had asked us once. A beat of outraged silence in the score. "This story is ABOUT," Heidi said, and the voice with its lion's mane became magnificent as she told the whole thing from beginning to end.

"Is she still a poet?" one of them had asked once. "We haven't seen her writing in a while." This struck me as the funniest thing I had ever heard; as if you could just stop being what you were. Maybe it's not set in the past, they suggested. Maybe it's set now, and she has to move back in with her parents because she gets sick. I thought about this for a long time before clearing my throat. But then none of the prog-rock references would work, I told them. There's this part where she's listening to King Crimson with her father in the car, and they raise their fists at the same moment and go AHHHHHHHHHH.

Had I not seen my father since my niece had died? He had insisted on having some sort of Latin singing at the funeral, by a guy who had never done it before, and it could only be described as *Gregorian mooing* or *cow chant*, and I could still see us all standing together, our shoulders shaking uncontrollably in the family pew. My father stood in front of us with a look of patient endurance on his face. He could have done the singing—if only, if only, he could have taken all the parts. How do you remember it all, I had never thought to ask; it is a performance, after all, a one-man show. And why hadn't I put it in, that he was the priest who rolled the whole Mass behind him in a suitcase, and set it up so carefully in my sister's hospital room?

"But that's so beautiful," Heidi said when I told her, and he rolled toward me for a moment holding hands with a younger self.

Next to me Mary stood tall. Her belief in cryptids was as perfect as ever—long necks in lakes, ape asses in the woods, leviathans. *Hogzilla*, she had sometimes called her daughter, in the Cajun accent of the man who believed that there was a four-thousand-pound pig hiding in the woods near his house. At night we watched *Oak Island*, a show where Canadian men dug forever in the mud. There was a legend that the Grail had gone to this place—the Grail never went to, like, New York. It went where people believed in it most, where people were willing to dig, and where Canada was not populated with identical interior decorators named Jnoathan, it was populated with amateur archaeologists. They scooped forever in the mud—sometimes they x-rayed the mud, as if it were a body—and when they found a button, they partied for days. To have found actual treasure, let alone the Grail, would have upset them. They were in it for the buttons and safety pins, for what the doctor called *Family History*.

Before the pitch, we had found a Catholic supply store where we picked out an olive-wood chalice. Summer of 2018, blacktop hot, and each of us wearing the other's clothes. We nodded at Werner Herzog as we passed him in the lobby (what kind of omen was Werner Herzog?), then stepped as one into the conference room, where I chugged an entire Red Bull from the cup without speaking and gestured at Heidi to begin. There was a question about the second season, the third. There are things that are happening in her life even now, Heidi said and hesitated, as I almost laughed. What was I, the fount of all happenings? I had seen it, in the body of my father—a whole country like my living room. You wanted this, I had choked out to my mother on the phone in my hotel room . . . you dragged me to those protests, you wanted all of this . . .

Patches of the air moved, as if the Predator were jumping from branch to branch. A priest groupie, who also appeared to be wearing a deep-sea fishing shirt, pulled a chair up to our table and sat on it backward. He nodded at me politely. Not knowing what was appropriate for the occasion, I myself had chosen a sloth halter and a kind of baby overall, and was carrying a little trash bag as a purse. The groupie leaned closer to my father and whispered something in his ear. My father leaned back and listened, one large and ready chuckle, part of the conspiracy.

I was afraid of hearing a name from his lips. The former president's. My own. I put in my earbuds and began playing rain sounds. These were supposed to soothe the nervous system, or allow you to feel that you were in a uterus again, or something. The new baby contemplated me over Mary's shoulder. He looked like a Victorian representation of the moon. For some reason I could not seem to *see* him. It was as if the part of the brain that registered the lower half of a person's face had been removed. I had noticed this and its strange converse: that sometimes, reconstructing a conversation with a person who was wearing a mask, my brain filled in their face as if they weren't, with what I was willing to bet was 100 percent accuracy.

Someone brought me a bratwurst. People kept bringing me foods my grandmother used to make. Why hadn't I put it in the book that my grandmother had died while it was all happening? That while my sister slept above us, I used to beg my mother in the downstairs kitchen to let my grandmother have more Marinol, a synthetic marijuana equivalent. "I *love* you," my grandmother told me, on Marinol, informing me, with eyes like large sweet scoops, that it was the last time, and later asking for ice cream. It had seemed like too much back then—no one would believe it. But that was before.

And after she had died, how we had gone through her brother's things. He had a farm just north of Cincinnati, with the creek running through it where we used to find fossils: horn coral, brachiopods, and once, something that looked like the human brain. I dreamed of that creek still. My great-uncle never seemed like a priest to me—he didn't wear day-to-day black—but there in that cardboard box was the evidence: a pectoral cross, a reliquary, a little leather flogger, and three plain gray rocks. I had taken pictures of everything and sent them to Heidi—in case we might find a use for them later, but really so I wouldn't forget. The kit seemed almost like something of mine, the little book, the rocks, the reverence, and how last summer, unable to understand anything and for the first time in my life, I had taken a hanger and beaten black stripes across my legs.

Something really had happened, finishing that first script. After a while it was like we were thinking through each other's hands. We typed the last bit, about rose petals falling from the ceiling, almost in alternating lines. Ceiling of the church, that is. The development team wanted so badly for me to become religious again, but save it, we thought, for season two or three, when I would become a priest in a rogue ordination ceremony held by radical nuns on a riverboat. Tradwives, trucker convoys, prairie hems, and head coverings—dirtbags who had somehow posted their way into a time before Vatican II—we had seen it all coming. We are the ones who can do this, we said, trading our clothes back and forth forever, though somehow the men in black kept getting all the good lines.

Tap tap tap. We loved to look things up instead of writing.

The little bits of business: her typing *folx* and me sneaking up to change it.

You don't have to write her getting *in*to the shower, she explained. You just have to show her getting out.

And her saying: I write because I hear voices.

I was writing about my mother and she was writing about her mother; I was writing about my father and she was writing about her father. At first it didn't work and then it did. We should do an episode where your dad goes on T! she said. Her father had gone on T and kept saying I feel GREAT! I feel GREAT! Almost impossible to write for my father if you had never met him, but after a while she had all of the voices—when she read his part, that's who I was, the daughter.

"Does that word look weird to you?" we said as we typed. Daughter. Daughters. Born on my birthday. The babies slept safely upstairs, in her house and in my mind.

The wind began to conduct the trees. The sky darkened and grew strange. There was a kind of stamping freedom, a madness in the mud, as something gathered over us. The children's cheeks glowed. Their teeth chattered in ecstasy; they had progressed beyond language. The bouncy house must have been to them like something in the clouds; they were launched by it, higher and higher, until you could see their curls in flung halos around their heads. Little bells tingled; the bread was being changed to pretzels, elephant ears, funnel cakes. What is Schutzenfest, I had kept asking, where will I be, but no one could tell me.

At all times it was like I had been transported elsewhere: mountain passes, winding trails, glacial faces. Or into another time: the hour before the earthquake, and I was all the animals. A vast overidentification marked me, with people, with landscapes, with tender bends in plants, as if I were a kudzu overtaking the earth. If I always knew when it was going to rain now, it was because beforehand I felt myself falling.

Someone brought me another bratwurst. Was a band playing, did I imagine it? One of those songs I found so exhilarating as an eight-year-old, like the one about it being Saturday in the park—could there be a more ecstatic scenario, than that it was Saturday, and we were in the park, and it might possibly be the Fourth of July? Perhaps the music was coming from inside the redbrick building, where the people who did not believe in death were. My sister had looked for an outdoor activity, a place we could gather together in safety; that was Schutzenfest. But inside, bunkered down, with bare faces—*singing*—is where my father wanted us; he kept surveying the outdoor melee and saying, "Ridiculous." It would be our fear that struck us, the thought that we could ever be vulnerable. But look at me, I thought to him, willing him to turn his eyes. I look like Nosferatu with Fly Girl bangs.

Like I drank from the wrong—like I had drunk from the wrong—I gave it to him afterward, the wooden one, and though it looked like all the humble ones you saw in the movies, the ones that wouldn't crumple you or turn you to gray dust, you could tell he didn't think it was real, not like the one with amethysts that he would lift into the light. Until I was seeing through sequins, high up. Now the angel was flapping in the corner of my eye, the prism was tearing its hole—a zigzag across the sky, I thought, that only my father and I could see. It began to rip the pattern of his deep-sea fishing shirt. It threatened to rip everything, even my Material. What had I told my husband recently? That I was experiencing *Permanent Visuals*. "Permanent Visuals?" he said. "That's like, being alive?"

But the pattern began to fall. I took out my Sounds to hear it. The rain was a body of pure touch, it fell on faces and faces alike, to turn them to concentric rings. The illumination must come as a surprise every time—I shine? I am in pieces? The great sound of cracking likewise, like a mast. That it fell on *Ohio* it would never have believed. This was a storm at sea.

The Great Flood must have had no idea, in the air, what it was there to do.

It wanted to wash us away. My father alone understood. He stood and pointed at the center pole. The camera framed him. Loaves and fishes seemed to shoot from a slit in his wrist—no, buns and bratwurst. "Twenty million volts!" he shouted. He glared at us, as if our inaction were the lightning bolt that would one day kill our mother. "I've seen people get struck by lightning on the golf course," he hissed, zooming in close to our faces, *"and let me tell you, it wasn't pretty."* He executed a sharp little spin, like a ballerina who was afraid of electricity, and strolled leisurely to the car to wait there, blasting music so progressive that its moment still hadn't arrived.

Ten pieces of water fell from the sky. Mary looked around cautiously. "It's like, drizzling," she said. "Am I insane?"

The camera watched him go. Illumination struck him again and again, the thing I had lately started calling *sighght*. God loved him, and he was in the process of being changed. Soon he would go Carnivore, and his hair would grow back, and he would be able to sing two steps higher—*there are things that are happening in his life even now*—"Listen," he would say to me earnestly on my birthday, and keep soaring up and up.

"Where did your father go?" my mother asked, returning with another bratwurst. "Mom, is Dad scared of lightning?" Mary asked. "OH YEAH," my mother told us in her OH YEAH voice. "Dogs, lightning, the devil, the number thirteen." And scanning the sky, she dashed after him through the mudhole, just as the real rain began to fall. We saw her zigzagging frantically through the parking lot, searching row after row for the two-door street-racing Audi that had been leased to him by a dealer who might have belonged to Opus Dei, until finally she came back to us streaming wet, with her hair plastered to her head like an otter. The fucker was completely dry, she informed us, raising her two middle fingers. She was up to her ankles in mud, mine. The Sounds had stopped, and would not begin again. It had rained for five minutes total, on Schutzenfest.

"Mom, did Dad ever see a man struck by lightning on the golf course?" I asked. "No, of course not," she said. "He's remembering *Caddyshack*."

End scene, I told Kurt Russell. Put it in the show, I thought, but who could ever play us.

A little tap dance had come through the phone as Heidi looked it up; we loved to look things up instead of writing. Her seltzer hissed in my ear as she took a sip and said, "Oh my God." The Cold War Reenactors Club actually existed—only fourteen members, but still active. We wouldn't use the scene, I knew, it was too late. They wouldn't pick up the show at all: radical nuns on a riverboat? But I had to hear that fresh drinking fountain voice lifting up and saying it again: "I . . . kind of love it."

Like my new bod?

"You can see it, can't you?" I asked Heidi, who wrote plays because she heard voices. Well now so did I too, finally. My mind unfolded metal chairs, struck the scene with a white all-comprehending light, laid my father down shaking in the middle of the aisle, gave him the opening that would allow all the rest of it to proceed in the proper way.

Be-ing A-live

The faces of the actors in *Original Cast Album: Company* were the faces of people in hell. Trying to achieve the definitive performance, staked to their own backbones inside a ring of flame. How their eyes emptied out and their souls exited through their mouths and how you did start to hear it, as soon as it began, the song that would be on the record. Something about it instantly printed, pressed, and the day was allowed to burn on.

How painful to be Stephen Sondheim, I thought, and have to rely on people for interpretation of works that stand perfect in the mind. It was like God, a pure gold scale, surrounded by children who were specially designed to scream every second they were alive. For a long time you couldn't find this movie; you had to hunt down clips of Elaine Stritch on YouTube, raking her claws through her hair as she did take after take, shouting at herself in a man's shirt, "STOP SCREAMING!" When she finally sticks the landing of "The Ladies Who Lunch," and Stephen Sondheim smiles, and it's the happiest he's ever been, and the last line just keeps shouting into the future: "RISE...RISE..."

"Am I Elaine Stritch?" I asked my husband.

"You're Stephen Sondheim."

"No, *you're* Stephen Sondheim."

"I just feel like Stephen Sondheim. But actually I'm nobody in this movie." He was being disingenuous. He kicked one leg in the air and screamed ahhhhhhHHHHLUNCH: a perfect impression. "What if you were the greatest actor of your generation?" I asked him—the freshest, the most creative, I had wondered it before—and he smiled, put his leg down, and closed his mouth on the secret; just like Elaine Stritch, pretending she didn't have it in her.

Dean Jones appeared on-screen. "I know this guy," he said, pointing. "Wasn't he..." But I was there ahead of him: Wikipedia. "Yes, he went method to play an evil veterinarian in the dog movie *Beethoven*," I recited, "and insisted on speaking in character the whole time it was filming, much to the surprise of his wife." Dean Jones held his shoulders like a sheet music salesman. Dean Jones held his shoulders like a piece of sheet music. He sang "Being Alive" once, serviceably—a song without fingerprints, whose own mother wouldn't recognize it. Stephen Sondheim asked him for another take and he grumbled that he had nothing left—the real version is like a dog named Beethoven, you must pretend you are not trying to catch it—then went helplessly to the microphone and opened his mouth....

And suddenly I knew more about Dean Jones than God, putting his little teeth in. The song took over and sang itself and that was the take. "Do I have to do everything?" it asked, secretly pleased. The air went in tune, the whole world went in tune—a flower pushed itself through the green fuse, an unbuttoned shirt tucked and straightened itself, somebody's nephew was born in Alaska. Stephen Sondheim always hated this ending. He wanted the main character to die choking on a big bite of birthday cake, the candles having set fire to his hair. But this is what wanted to happen instead, what wanted to happen was the song. The song cleared its throat so completely that it disappeared, the throat that was Dean Jones.

    I alone in the whole world was watching him. He was wearing a red turtleneck and looked familiar, like someone who had appeared in a bunch of Disney movies about million-dollar ducks, which in fact he had. Something was shaking Dean Jones by the shoulders; his mother; it was Sunday morning and he had the solo. He opened wider, he began to turn inside out, until I saw his uvula and his fillings and the ribs of a church ceiling, and then I was dissolving like sugar against the roof of his mouth and that was the take, the permanent take. He closed his mouth on "Being Alive" and I saw him blinking out forty-five years in the future. Dean Jones left the show after opening night. In ten years God would lift his black moods from him. He became a Christian, and tried to star in a musical about the Shroud of Turin—"called Into the Light!" I screamed, "*Into the Light!*"—which closed after six performances, but there it was against me, printed: the sweat of a face.

Shakespeare's Wife

A warm afternoon in winter, and Shakespeare's wife was asking to see me. She wanted to buy my brain, but how to explain that it was no longer worth anything?

Someone had texted the wrong time, so I walked into the corner restaurant five minutes late, rehearsing her alias, which meant something in Greek. The maître d' had no idea what I was talking about, and instead led me to a small glass greenhouse outside—where I sat considering the salt, and beginning to burn like a prism, till she appeared in front of me lit from behind, saying, "I thought we might be in two different places." She took me to a back table, where she had been serenely overlooking a dumpster full of mannequin parts. "I can't remember the last time I had twenty minutes to myself," she said, a shoal of fragile colors assembling into her profile. "It made me realize that what I really need is an office," where presumably the dumpster full of mannequin parts would be moved for her contemplation.

She was looking very beautiful, for Shakespeare's wife. I asked her if she was psychic and she said, "I know when people are going to die." Regarding her past lives, she knew only that she was a gentleman who had been murdered. "I can feel the tip of the knife pressing into my back. But *you*," she said, pointing a finger at me, "are not a baby like you think, but something very old that is living a human life for the first time. Like a mountain. Or a stone." Late in life, she had finally unlocked the secret to her dancing: She wasn't using her left heel. "Oh yes," I said. "I know all about that. My dancer friend tells me I make too many triangles." She nodded as if that were a well-known pitfall, and both of us turned to the dumpster then, where legs kicked in a free chorus line.

She was dressed as an equestrian and I was dressed as a female centaur; our turtlenecks were so total that it was a wonder either of us could breathe. We sipped espresso and agreed that if we were young now, we would be both agender and poly. "I would be . . . everything," she said with a hand wave, looking out the window. While she was distracted, I scrambled six huge bites of omelet into my mouth. She had ordered avocado toast and managed, by some feat of pantomime, to make it smaller without eating any at all; she had unlocked left heels in her body that I didn't even know about.

I was having a Protagonist Problem: I could not move, or make anything happen. Were we in a kind of place that would keep going, like a stage. It seemed we would die before ever discussing the thing we had come there to discuss. Adaptation, I thought, like a writer or an animal. I had written down our first conversation months ago, so I would be sure to remember it—everything about it, down to the pauses, and her excellent William H. Macy impression. "Straightforward Reportage of a Conversation with Shakespeare's Wife," I called it. And a violet scarf tied around her neck, neatly holding both of our heads on.

She talked about the center path. She said that last night she had gone to a rave that started at six p.m., but the bouncer told her that she was too early. She told me she pictured the first half as a rave, with music thumping and huge screens. She said she thought there should be an arc where everyone in the world was following a story about an animal, perhaps an animal in grief—"a baby elephant in Kenya who keeps returning to the same site."

She said she was a "physics freak" and mentioned fractals. She said that she and Jared Leto are both "you can never step in the same river twice" actors. She liked the bit about the name tag . . . was she born as Shakespeare's wife? She liked the bit about the vagina egg and she said that she had tried to put a storyline in her current show about [*famous actress made of vegetables*] reaching in to adjust her vagina egg but legal refused to clear it. That was pretty funny, I thought.

"Did she play you techno?" my husband asked afterward. She played me techno. She said, "Here's what I think about religion. Hey man. People are just trying to get closer to God!" She kind of yelled that last part. "I am obsessed with Madonna"—no, I am obsessed with *the* Madonna. She had connected to the material because . . . and here she turned to show me a painting of a butterfly sitting on a Corvette. The Corvette must have been her body, but it seemed like a secret to hear why the butterfly was black. What I had written seemed like a secret too.

The book was unfilmable—we both knew that, of course. It really couldn't be done. There was a baby who needed to be born in it, who could not be depicted. But she was so brave. She made her voice so strong and swinging as she explained how we would do it. "It's simple. We build . . ." My heart rate, when I checked it later, dropped to forty-eight beats a minute. At the end of the conversation, like pregnant women, we both had to pee at the same time.

Children who were born and children who were not born. I sipped more espresso, became temporarily alive, and felt a brief pang in my lower belly for the man who was competing with Shakespeare's wife to buy my brain. He looked kind and spent and sad, like a vegetarian vampire. He had never staged a play before, but he said to me, "I see it." There were ways to do the baby onstage—a light behind a white sheet, for example. A Calder mobile of stars and Lucite organs. A French shadow puppeteer, ninety-eight years old, about to expire and take all his secrets with him. And to hold her? "We could hire the best actress in the world," he told me, laughing, "or you could do it."

I had been picturing something different: me as the god in street clothes, Joan Didion with a carton of soup between rehearsals. But for a moment it seemed possible, a spotlight in the center of the stage, white hallways of the hospital, scattered cries, the nurse named *Janet*, me walking slowly toward the prism that was burning in the glass greenhouse—lifting it away from the monitors and into my arms. "It's just that I see it," he said to me, almost frustrated, rubbing the thinking lines in his forehead. "Sometimes that happens. I read something and I see it." I knew what he meant—you were reading and suddenly the play was on its feet, an organism with head, heart, hands, lust, thirst; people in black moving mountains back and forth, quick changes in the wings, the heave of red velvet, and suddenly: Lady Hamlet holding up her own skull onstage. We get the best actress in the world, or you could do it. And once wasn't enough? Every night? Every night?

"Or you could have been a river," Shakespeare's wife said now, downstairs in the bathroom of the restaurant, as we were peeing next to each other in adjacent stalls. She was being polite, because I went for such a long time that it started to seem like I would never stop, a thing I was famous for among those who knew me. Jared Leto would go crazy. He would step and step and step.

The Character has to want something, and she has to change. "What are you afraid of?" she had asked me, above—as someone must ask before you are born again. Two hours had passed and I still hadn't answered. Holding it all up, every night, every night. Having it happen again, and to me. Shakespeare's wife startling awake with her secret knowledge, and Shakespeare lying next to her going *What? What? What?* We walked out of the bathroom and up into the sunshine. I carried the stone she had given me, which claimed to connect heaven and earth. I passed the dumpster, where the legs were unlocking their left heels, where the hands were raised in gesture and the great white heads were glowing, and a tenderness overcame me for the ones who played us on the stage of the world. I could let go, I thought, and let someone else say my lines. I could let someone else wear my clothes. Not a baby like I thought, but something very old living a human life for the first time.

Boys Over Flowers

Maybe you could die in one country and wake up in another. Maybe you could start over, speaking something other than English.

We started watching dramas because my husband had grown up in Yeonhui-dong, and I wanted him to see it again. At first he wasn't interested—he hated all television that wasn't men climbing mountains—but soon, "That's Lotte World!" he would cry. "The 63 Building! Itaewon!" I've been there, he would say; I've eaten that. There's an aquarium in the basement of that mall, with live mermaids. The uphill streets, the bisecting river. Seoul. After a while, we kept watching because I thought of it as the place where my husband was still alive.

"It's that cold in winter," he would say, watching clouds come from the actors' mouths. You could get hot drinks from vending machines, he told me, and buy baked potatoes on the street. But other things we learned for the first time: how to make hangover soup, to order a fruit plate with your cocktails in the hotel bar. How to pour soju for someone, and how to keep both hands on the glass, and turn away as you sipped it. Actually I began to drink a bit again, then stopped, and that was fine; apparently I could no longer process it, and turned so purple I had to go to the doctor.

The shows often involved orphans. They often involved "third-generation chaebols," which was one of the most satisfying phrases in any language to say. Frequently it turned out that the two main characters had met as children, and were each other's destiny. "How do you not remember him?" we would yell at the TV. "You met him on a suspension bridge in Switzerland! He lived with your family for six months in the eighties! She killed a butterfly right in front of you on the day that your mother was murdered!" Yet the tropes seemed to sleep somewhere inside him. A man dropped a little key chain on the floor of a hotel room where he was trying to cheat on his wife. "Aha," he chortled, "*the marriage jangler . . .*"

I had grown up with a photographic memory for faces, but after I was sick had a hard time recognizing British and American ones, possibly because the language was attached to them. But here I found my ability intact again—I could spot a man who appeared in one scene of *Secret Garden* as the man who gets comic back surgery in *Sky Castle*. "It's him," I would insist, and I was always right. That's the child with the bowl cut. That's the secretary with diarrhea. Diarrhea was occasionally used as a plot point, which felt more like real life. Hadn't my own mother been struck with it after a fried chicken dinner on a road trip, and had to be driven by total strangers to an ER in Indiana— back when I was little, and had a bowl cut myself?

The inability to process narrative, my disorientation at fast cuts, the unzipping inside my skull whenever the camera moved diagonally—

all of these went away. The shows were brighter, and often rested on faces. *Coffee Prince, My Mister, Goblin.* It should be like that, I thought. Words written under people. For some reason I could *follow* again. I could remember that that was the guy who developed autistic symptoms after the car crash and now retreated to the woods to play his violin; wasn't this basically what had happened to me? All the other information was available too. This is what people were wearing in 2008. All the men used to have their left ears pierced, you could still see the holes. A whole country and its history were in evidence, in the form of Hyun Bin pretending to swap bodies with a stuntwoman.

The summer before, I had tried to rewire my brain with mushrooms, but succeeded mainly in becoming temporarily psychic and reading *Anna Karenina* so hard I almost died. But watching the dramas, these acquisitions were almost accidental, as if my brain had become plastic again. At first I could only catch family names—oma, oppa, halmoni, unni, hyung—then thank you, and I'm sorry, and I love you. One of the nights I had been drinking I had heard it, the language separating into units. It was like suddenly realizing you could read. "I can hear it!" I cried, completely purple, and called my husband a crazy bastard.

Fandom, which I had never understood, must be a way to organize life, longing, and a desire to look things up on the internet—three things that were too large otherwise. You couldn't choose what you liked best, it was more like that *New York Times* experiment where you looked into someone's eyes for twenty minutes and accidentally pair-bonded like a penguin. The screen filled with faces, the whole world translated through faces. "Those two got married," my husband said, pointing at the screen. "That means that the whole time they were filming, they were in love. Oh my God," he whispered, looking at his phone, "she's pregnant...."

After a while you knew some of the myths. You knew about the Granny who was in charge of who was born, and you knew about nine-tailed foxes and the different rules for ghosts, and you knew the name of the river the dead crossed and what buckwheat flowers meant. These made a difference in what was possible. American shows, which rarely involved rebirth either at the beginning or the end, seemed to close their eyes to a deep blue dimension where more of the story could take place—uphill streets, bisecting river; Seoul, the city where my husband was still alive.

And somewhere in the future, his wonderful mother saying: *I hope I did everything I could to make sure you were safe while you were still inside me.* . . .

Three quarters of the way through, the actors would be exhausted: five o'clock shadows, breakouts along the jawline, haircuts a quarter-inch too long. That's where we are now, I told myself, but it won't last forever. We will be refreshed, once the drama is over. At some point, no matter what else was happening, someone always ended up in the hospital—"Humidifier!" my husband would cry, pointing, and, "That's where my broken arm was set! That's where I was tear-gassed by police while going into Hankook to be vaccinated!" We were two episodes into *Crash Landing on You* when he doubled over on the plane and we had to rush him to the hospital from Heathrow. We were six episodes in when he collapsed buying orange juice at Hudson News and we had to rush him to the hospital from JFK. When they strapped him to the stretcher and lifted him into the ambulance, I could not think what to do, *it was his life*. My mouth was empty, and my brain was like the moment when the subtitles gap out—pure terror, what was happening, would I never understand anything again? Every gesture in the world was gone from my body. How do I tell him, I thought, how do I tell him? My husband, when I looked at him, was holding up finger hearts.

Part Three

Hidden Track

Because the whole row had been left to her—actually the whole section—because she may herself have been a ghost on that plane, and the plane itself a ghost—she was able to put up the armrests and lie back with her knees up and her feet in their tie-dyed socks on the seat, wrapped firmly in a blanket so no one could take a picture of her while she was sleeping and post it with a derogatory caption. The socks were a gesture to her youth, the silence and red darkness surrounding her were amniotic, and all that flashed on her were occasional images from *Mrs. Doubtfire*, which her husband was watching in the row ahead of her.

She was listening to an album that she could only ever listen to alone. The first five notes pressed down keys in her chest, and then the synthesized sound of the singer's voice began wobbling up like bubbles. The cover of the album was mountains, so she was sliding up and down those with the music, while at the same time her inner chess piece was trying to open the doors, where, to the place where she had originally bought the album. She could see herself in the section—alternative? Electronic? Wearing, what, a winter peacoat? If I could just put myself back in my clothes, she thought, I could get there, I could buy it again.

"Everything feels like drag to me," she remembered telling the doctor, as Robin Williams wrestled himself into his false torso, as he zipped up a flowered dress, as he rose up with his face covered in whipped cream, shouting HELLO! Her husband had interviewed Robin Williams once, and after asking him a series of too-intense questions about the forearm prosthetics he had worn in the movie *Popeye*, he had said "Thank you" and made to hang up the phone, when Robin Williams asked almost plaintively, "Wait . . . don't you want to hear about what I'm doing now?" and soon afterward he had died, so that her husband had never been able to untangle the two, and carried a great guilt for a long time, thinking that if he had asked the question, maybe it wouldn't have happened. "But this is the problem *I* have," she had told him earnestly, "that I think I control the world, that I'm keeping the plane up with my mind."

Why didn't anyone recognize Mrs. Doubtfire? Everyone was either her child or her wife. One hip rose into a great hill of pain, and all she was thinking for a moment was who had chosen the seat upholstery. She was flying Virgin, just as she had been back then, and with that word she was back in the listening booth, alone. Her brain was falling through the back of her head as through a trap door, sometimes plummeting free, sometimes catching and sinking through a smaller dense cloud; the album had been described as difficult, but it had never felt that way to her. One of her eyelids drooped down with the singer's, in sympathy. She dozed off for a moment, her mouth wide open behind her mask, and came to again with a gasp.

Why didn't anyone recognize Mrs. Doubtfire? Her eyes were the same, her mouth was the same, everything was so familiar until it wasn't, a hidden track had begun playing—how—in the album she had heard a thousand times before. Now the singer was unzipping a long skin suit, wrestling his slim shoulders out, and stepping upward. He was walking toward her through the landscape as volcanoes rose around him, like the creation of the world in a single person, which she supposed it was again, every time. The tender bullseye in the center of her chest was being struck and struck—how lucky—there was music like that out there that she had never heard, most of it had never been recorded, a recent movement of internet weirdos had banded together to listen to less, it was everywhere, they complained, people were not meant to listen to so much music, in the past, people had never listened to music alone.

She woke up and it was over. The one walking toward her was not the singer at all, but her husband, clutching his lower belly, white, strange, unhimself, swaying. The hidden track had closed itself, the credits were playing, and everyone knew who Mrs. Doubtfire was. Fan theory went that the hidden track depicted the person from the previous song, "Motion Picture Soundtrack," transcending into the afterlife. Many others described their surprise—surely it hadn't been there before, that door? In the place where music went on it was happening over and over, a person stepping off the top step into space, out of the past and their life and into—don't you want to know what I'm doing now?

Life-and-Death

The first surgery had gone perfectly. Laparoscopic, performed by a robot that she pictured as a mechanical spider, six neat slits up and down his abdomen and like that: half of the thing called guts gone. "If I ever want to quit, I could go back and watch a video of that," the surgeon said to her in the waiting area, six foot three in scrubs, his height seeming to climb the trunk of an immense satisfaction, his nose sunburned from some perpetual afternoon on a boat. Actually he had retired at some point, and then, addicted to the race car thrill of Bowels, still feeling the warmth of the steering wheel in his hands, he had returned—to be here with her, rocked back on his heels, telling her it went about as perfect as it could go.

But when they wheeled her husband back into the recovery room, he had begun to cry out. "I feel like a 180-pound man is standing on me"; the 180-pound man was himself. It's not possible, they kept telling him, wheeling in the X-ray machine to reassure him, There's nothing there now. If the physical therapists had come to walk him that afternoon, the blood would have poured out then. But it waited, filling him up, in a different way than blood fills us up usually.

He called them his slaughterhouses. "I had two slaughterhouses, one at eleven thirty p.m. and one at five thirty-three a.m." He said it was like *The Shining*, a crashing floor of red. "I think you're going to have to save my life," he told the night nurse, after the second slaughterhouse, and then the hospital went into action like a body gathering itself to kick. It was then that her phone began to ring, on the pillow next to her head, in their faraway house on the islands. The voice of the emergency doctor began, "Your husband . . . ," that word she had always found funny. "You seriously think I have a husband?" she always thought, when anyone said it to her. But then the words *going in again*.

She called a friend who woke every morning at that time to write. "The water is low," they said automatically, as they drove over the marshes. She pressed the gas when he pressed the gas, hung right when he hung right, the route to her husband flying inside her as if it could make her faster: hit the pavement, on through the double doors, grab two masks from the dispenser, past the gift shop, the good bathroom where she overheard night nurses talk about how *the joy was gone*, past the Starbucks to the elevator and hold your breath all the way upstairs.

Running, as she had once run toward him in the airport, though unable at the last moment to make the leap into his arms.

He had lost two liters and another liter waited inside him. When she walked into the room, she felt a presence. Was it the smell of all that blood? Was it the Man in the Hat, that children saw when they took Benadryl? "I think I'm delirious," the night nurse said, taking down her mask to cough. All that bending over to mop the floor—housekeeping wasn't allowed to clean blood. So it would stay, splashed on the baseboards and the underside of the chair, as long as they were in 373. Maybe it would always be there.

"I can't believe you made it," he said, as if she had completed the leap and he were holding her. Before they brought him back for the second round of anesthesia, she was allowed to sit pressing his hand in a little cubicle. He was very, very cold, like a sculpture in progress. She signed something, she didn't know what. Then the waiting room, with the woman at the intake desk remembering her, and the screen with the names of those *In Progress* and *In Recovery*, and the milling Starbucks in the center that seemed to be life itself. The sharp-edged smell of coffee, like brain surgery. Five hours of the detective show *Monk*, so that at some point she passed into a plane of reality that contained only the obsessive-compulsive show *Monk*, with her husband being meticulously operated on in a room off to one side. At one point KoRn appeared as guest stars, and a portion of the episode took place on their tour bus. She screenshotted Jonathan Davis's white dreads like crazy, as a form of hope. He would make it. She would show him.

The surgeon, when he came to speak to her, was baffled. If he could only say two words, he would say *the damnedest*. "One day we'll look back and say, Well, that's not how that was supposed to go," said the surgeon, the wind of the perpetual afternoon shearing past him. Luck his whole life had been with him—he had done more than twenty-five hundred of these surgeries, and had only had to open someone up again twice. "I had to cut him open this time," he apologized, making a vertical incision in the air; there was so much blood, and the robot sat powered down in the corner, ashamed. "I'm sorry about that. But I gave him some of that good fresh frozen plasma."

Her friend, the writer, stood with her as she had requested, in case she forgot to ask something important. She listened to the surgeon in her way that was not listening, drawing the curls on his temples with her eyes—wondering what the *S*. of his first name stood for, then writing a beautiful *S* on the palm of her hand like Annie Sullivan. When he was finished, she turned to her friend with her mouth open, the phrase *good fresh frozen plasma* still sliding down her throat. He turned to address the surgeon. "What *happened?*" he said.

"What I think now," her husband said in a voice so clear it seemed to proceed from his saline drip, "is that humans are amazing." He had never said anything of the kind before.

> *I prayed,* he said
> <*Who did you pray to?*>
> *Ganesh, Christian god, ancestors*
> *Oh, I did Jah, too*
> *World mother? Gaia*
> *Also aliens*

All animals, he told her, all universes, crisscrossed and became one. Morphine and Dilaudid, fentanyl, gabapentin; two rounds of anesthesia in three days. He was experiencing closed-eye visuals: the moment he closed his eyes on the hospital pillow he began to recite, in a ticker-tape voice, what he could see. It was important to remember, she thought, but he was in that state where contact with her hand kept him in contact with the world, where otherwise he would disperse in flocks, and over the backs of horses. So she stayed hunched forward holding his hand, as doctors and nurses passed in and out, and she pressed the button for more morphine whenever he drowsed awake and asked *how much time she had left on her frog.*

> *And I saw Rio de Janeiro*
> *Now I see a platypus's foot*
> *I see pine trees—what is that—jellyfish*
> *Little crabs*
> *A big mustache flying around*
> *Old Western steak restaurant, a proto-Sizzler*
> *Two Native Americans kissing. Male*
> *Textures* he said

That night she slept in the chair splashed in blood. He had become afraid not of the dark, but of night, the time when it happened. And if she had not left the hospital after the first surgery, had not eaten a sandwich at home, had not fallen asleep in the middle of the bed, kicking out her selfish legs . . . ? She closed her eyes and saw the Rothko, one rectangle of red on top of another. In order to know how really beautiful it was, you had to be in the same room with it. Why see the Rothko at this time, but that's what the Rothkos were waiting for. Inside you. He slept. Then there was the Hockney exhibit, still cool pools in paradise. A surgeon in the bath with a little sailboat toy; ten-foot-tall waves, and in the end he saves it.

Her husband's father, put together upside down, seemed to be walking toward her. He had called with a dream shortly before he died, had asked to speak to her specifically: A spotted horse was walking through the desert, and every time he bent to drink, all of his spots disappeared. That's the Bible, she thought, just as he said, "I thought you could use it in your writing." But then the window lightened and she saw it was the surgeon, fresh like plasma from saving some other life. Later her husband would make an identical incision in the air, up his abdomen and across, accompanied by that water-droplet noise in his cheek that some boys—never girls—were able to make. The satisfaction he took in this gesture, in this sound, must have been imparted by the surgeon, a father of a kind.

"It has long been accepted as scientific fact that reality is organized into a series of layers." He woke one morning with this written in a Notes file. "All of the layers are made of materiality. And the materiality of each layer is shared by everything that originates from that layer, but is separate from the materiality of every other layer.

"But all of the layers drip and splash, so sometimes a drip or splash of materiality from one layer bumps against another.

"These are the layers that we have so far: There is the Yellow Layer, which is the one that I am on. There is the Fish Layer, also known as the Blue Layer. There is the Spirit Layer, and there is the God Layer. The God Layer is occupied by a single entity called God, whose materiality stretches infinitely and fills its whole layer. The God Layer is the only layer that's self-aware. If you ask it a question, it always replies: I am a system. Recently the God Layer has developed the ability to control some of its drips and splashes onto others.

"The people and things that occupy the Yellow Layer are now experimenting with a new technology called Drip-Glider that has the ability to catch a drip and follow it into other layers but so far this is only theory."

It was so funny, the sound of it—why did new religions always sound like that?—until you realized it was the clarity of a man beginning to starve. It had now been seven days since he had eaten, and his thoughts had climbed up into a thin white air. "Please," he said to anyone who came into the room, "please," but his NG tube was still bringing up bile, and they didn't want to introduce a new line because of the possibility of infection.

"Talk to people, please," he said restlessly, so she turned on *The Golden Girls*, who sat in their quilted nightgowns around the kitchen table that looked like the one in the old rectory, and sliced the white cheesecake of the clock over and over. "Please," he said, "fill the room with people," and she looked around and her mother and father walked in the door. They counted as people, though she could not tell to which layer they belonged. Fish, Yellow? Not the God layer, since that was self-aware.

This seemed to rest him and he slept. In the darkness, her mother told the story of a doctor bombarding her father with gamma rays when he was five years old, to stop him from going deaf. To stop the *ossification*, her mother said. The little hammers and anvils in his ear were turning to stone. It worked, she said, and her voice became triumphant. When he tried to join the navy at eighteen, the doctor had to write a letter telling what he had done, but refused to sign it, fearing liability. "*The navy eventually determined that nothing they did could increase the level of radiation in your father's body*," she said.

This was one of her mother's sentences; delivered of it, she then left to eat lunch for four hours. No one knew where she went at these times—through a wormhole, into the other world? It was a philosophical question, like peekaboo. "Have you ever heard that story before?" her husband asked when he woke up; he hadn't been gone when he was gone. There was a drop of blood still crusted on his earlobe from the glucose test; she caught it and followed it into the other layer, where they worked over him forever. And why hadn't it been his time? "She is the only thing keeping me on this earth," he told her, pointing to the sluttiest Golden Girl.

Her father sat in the chair that was splashed with blood and filled one corner of the room with his hammers and anvils and his levels of radiation that nothing could increase. He had, her mother had reported, gone Carnivore, and now took a sixty-dollar potassium supplement that was endorsed by a YouTube chiropractor called Dr. Berg (related searches *is dr berg a real doctor, is dr berg a scientologist*). He feasted seven days a week at Texas Roadhouse—a people company that just happened to serve steaks—and watched videos in his free time about how plants were poisonous to us, often appearing in the dining room while the family was eating salads to yell at them about it. "He never felt better in his life."

"It means so much to me that you came," her husband told her father from the hospital bed, in the voice of the saline drip, and he had never said anything like that before either.

"I just feel so bad for him," she cried to her parents at Sorry Charlie's Oyster Bar, where her father escorted them after visiting hours for the Carnivore meal that was his nightly requirement. It was possibly the most emotion she had ever displayed to them—that was all right, they would be leaving the next morning anyway, for a submarine reunion in Norfolk. The town, orbiting its central fountain through the window, looked like it had when she and her husband first visited and decided on a whim to live there. I could just do this, at any time, she thought, watching from a distance as a drop splashed from another layer. I could put my face in my hands and cry. Her father gazed at her with a spaniel's compassion, then mournfully threw back his head as he took a shot of hot-sauce butter. And kept to himself the unkind thought: It had been the plants that did it.

Thirty-six staples, and a few of them just above the belly button were opening. There was an eye of blood now on the bedsheets, and sometimes a little yellow on the gauze. This always happened with vertical incisions—the body, the on-call doctor explained, wanted to open up from side to side, and she imagined herself having a Christian feeling about the way he held out his arms. Irritated, he made a special note in the chart that the dressing must be changed every day, but when the nurse read it, she shook her head briskly. "I'll let him deal with that tomorrow," she said, either Australian or in possession of a speech impediment.

They could bring him food again, or cheerful liquids. Apple juice and chicken broth and orange Jell-O—he wouldn't have the red in case it came out of him looking like blood. "That was like a feeling I remember," he said in awe, the first time the nurse came in to change his diaper. "From being a baby. Swear to God it was like my earliest memory just got uncovered." A maniacal optimism, like the one that had led her to screenshot the white dreads of the lead singer of KoRn, led them to bring him a tray containing an entire roast turkey dinner. Well. She was never going to let a turkey dinner just sit there. She ate it.

The blood splashed and splashed on the underside of her chair. A bank of black clouds rolled in from the east. What were these states she was lifted into, by the throat, by the hair, into a weird white sky? Was physical insanity possible, could the back of the neck be insane? Was she suffering from roller coaster, from treetop, from rope bridge? What was it? Everything at once? *Textures?*

"The rain . . ." her husband said, pointing out the window. It was going to fall, but first it had to pull them up in parts . . . what did she think the rain *was* . . . in the middle of the air, were atoms marshaling to heal him . . . the whole world of atoms, though they had refused to heal others . . . and how afterward, could you stop feeling chosen, as if you were the thing that opened the flowers.

"You stopped writing poetry?" she imagined the doctor asking.

"I could no longer bear," she said, holding out her changed hands, "the *form*." It was the drop from one line to another, and the little noun hanging on its own. Poems were—which she had liked before—not possible, not possible, not possible, not possible. "What do you see?" she asked her husband, her finger on the button waiting to record.

I saw four or five thousand things that I've never seen before, in incredible detail, from other planes and realities. <And everything was crisscrossing?> Everything was in one place all of a sudden. <Like a physical point?> We were just all together. <We were all together.> I had no physical feelings or sensation, I was totally removed from everything except like sight and sound. <Pause.> And my third eye reaching out.

<Do you feel like you had a third eye then?> I feel like it must be there, I just don't normally have access to it. <But now you believe in the third eye.> I believe in everything now.

"Take a picture," he said, "take a picture," and gathered her to him with his long right arm. "Take a video of me walking down the hall," and she followed, trying to censor his ethereal ass through the back of his green gown; the ethereal ass, he had told her, that the charge nurse had turned over to take a picture of that night, to convince the surgeon to come. When she clicked on his face in Photos, her phone played a long memory of everything they had ever experienced, ending with a picture of him sitting on the toilet in room 373. Forgetting that he wasn't allowed to laugh, she texted it to him. "Ah. Ah. Ah. Ah. Ah. Ah. Ah," he said. Are you in pain? she asked. No. New laugh.

"You might not have a belly button when this is over," someone told him. The pulled staples had become a Wound. They brought in a specialist to look at him, who lifted the dressing, blanched, and began to pull more staples. The longer people stayed in hospitals, the worse things were for them—and it was true that now when her husband said, "Take a picture!" she could hardly bear to look. His cheekbones came closer and closer. There was a photograph of his grandmother standing on a porch in Oklahoma, like a skull looking out through a William Morris pattern. She had died after a routine gallbladder surgery, showering, on the morning she was supposed to leave.

"We're getting you out of here," the specialist told him. *"You are not doing well in here."* She knew that—what could she do? They had become Disaster People. At some point they had stopped living life, and started living something called Life-and-Death. How could she help him, what could she do? Blood, bones, wounds—she had used these things. You don't understand, she heard herself explaining to his body, don't you know that you're a *metaphor*?

In readiness she gathered up the flowers, cards; Mang-tae from the gift shop and the other stuffed animals; the bouquet of balloons from her little brother, along with his tips on wound care. She switched away from *Golden Girls*, passed *Ghost Hunters* ("No!" he squeaked. "No!!"), and settled on a three-hour marathon of a reality show about people pimping out aquariums. They were spray-painting coral forms, sourcing sunken anchors, measuring temperature and salinity. They were always on the phone, yelling things like: "Lil Jon is gonna need those betta fish before his comeback show opens in Vegas!" Fish tanks were so eighties, like him, like her. They kept having to manufacture crises with the aquariums, but the only crisis with an aquarium could be: It spilled.

They filled it again. They pumped gallon after gallon. The rectangles, the Rothko, the Hockney. An aquarium in the basement of him—in Seoul—with live mermaids. "It sounds insane," he told her, as someone knocked on the door to release him, "but I swear I'm having memories from the blood of the people they gave me." Just a glimpse from time to time, he said, slowly rising. Just a ten-foot-tall wave . . . someone in the bath . . . a sailboat toy . . . She took his arm and walked him out. The death of his death had been in that room.

The Wound

He never mentioned the Red Layer, but that must have been the one she was on. "You're in charge of the Wound," he said as they left the hospital on the twelfth day. Finally, a place to put her conscientiousness! At last, a place to put getting it perfect!

"I think I can look at it," he said as she helped him out of the shower. According to the scale he weighed 140 pounds; his Christ now belonged to the Middle Ages, rather than the Renaissance. He took a breath and he looked and then he vacated himself like a chameleon in the desert. His whole face slid up the mirror and he fainted. He slumped against the toilet as she held him up; his strength had gone inside her. What do you do? You think to yourself the words *sal volatile*, and then you slap his face. She braced him between the wall and the trash can—both of them had the idea that if he hit the ground he would come apart in two pieces, like one of the test melons on *Forged in Fire*—and then edged into the hall to hook her foot around one leg of his walker. She could hear herself saying something over and over. "*OK OK OK OK,*" she said.

His mouth gaped. His pupils puddled and spread in different directions. She helped him down the hall, standing straighter than she ever had: She was in charge of the Wound. They had agreed that she would change the dressing in a front bedroom they always kept closed—the air was stale, and the light bulb sizzled, and a former Chihuahua had made mistakes all over the carpet. "Are you ready?" she asked, and he nodded. Bare white sheet, the first time. He lay down on the bed and unwrapped his robe.

So that's what the inside of her husband looked like. Red layers, a taut opening, and a sort of inner glistening. A shape like a buttonhole, and "You missed one," she might have said, had it been anything other than himself. And smiled into it as she did him up, with that special look of wives—you would fall apart without me, can't do anything for yourself.

Like this? her whole body asked, bent over him like a question mark. One by one she took up the angled scissors, and the long-stemmed Q-tip, and the bottle of saline, and the squares of gauze. The terms united with what she was doing: She *packed it wet to dry* as if she were qualified. They had just let them go home like that. A husband could *just be open like that?* Two or three inches, a sideways eye? She could simply put her hand in him, as if this whole thing were religious? Or . . . a sort of vagina, after all?

It is difficult to describe, but at first it was dead. It wasn't *doing* anything; it just lay there. Everywhere she looked—his arms, torso, pelvis—her eyes seemed to be resting on the place the statue stopped. Broken off or bleached. It seemed like Zeno had been put in charge, as if the weapon that had struck the wound were still in the air. Then it began to interact with her.

You had to leave it alone a little bit, she realized. Let it work in the night, like the unconscious. A Benzedrine, a black coffee, a walk in the woods; then lunch and a nap and the proof woke up solved. Pringo, she thought, though that was not quite the word. Close your eyes, she had told him in the hospital, as the workings of the universe went on in him:

> *I'm in a gondola I'm looking at gravel pomegranate seeds rolling down into a gutter a man emptying a city trash can full of giant beetles a mountain of dinosaur skin, rolling along the landscape and incorporating pieces of metal.*

What I think now is that humans are amazing. Maybe he had seen them from above as a Closed-Eye Visual, working all together like an anthill, a texture. Smooth heads of hair joined in industry, hands flashing down a long piano, stitching the grass with sterile needles—as the two circular staples had joined him together again, deep in the earth below the incision, like wedding rings thrown into a volcano.

"There was a nurse," he drowsed in her arms, cool as he always was now; "I don't want to misgender. I decided they were the kindest and the gentlest. They sat with me for the longest time that night, holding my hand. Someone came looking for them at some point, but I think I didn't want to let them stop holding my hand."

When she closed her own eyes, long past his, her fingers fluttered among it, attending. Measuring its depth. Disinfecting the surgical scissors. Drawing on a pair of lilac gloves, asking herself whether they weren't actually *orchid*. Rationing her movements to the millimeter—the opposite of her roamings on his body in bed, her hand moving in helpless roses on his shoulder, as if there were not enough: of her, or him, and they were running out of each other.

At the time she was reading little sentences of Proust, as translated by Lydia Davis. These sentences also had slits, paper cuts, stitches; they healed and then opened again. It did not escape her that the main thing doctors had told her to look for was the smell, which might become the whole memory later. Fish, or death, is what they said, laughing. But from other wounds, she knew from her childhood reading, there came the smell of flowers.

"*Remembrance of Things Past?*" her teacher had asked in high school, and up shot her hand on the instant—again, that sense of ownership over books she had only heard of. "Remember the part where he tastes the madeleine?" the teacher said, miming a dipping motion. "No," she said baldly. Never would she tell a better joke. "Remember *memory*?" the teacher might as well have said—but the dipping motion stayed with her, it went into the Wound. She imagined it healing in different ways: a straight line or a crooked one, purple or pale, dependent on her passionate and scholarly attention. For a long time I used to go to bed early. Time and again, I have gone to bed early. Time was when I always went to bed early. And going in to the body and coming out rested.

Tell me about the memories, she said, when he had the feeling of other blood coursing through him. Someone else, he said. I think I lived over near Waters. A man, I know I was a man. Her sister saying, *This is actually in the literature, someone gets a kidney transplant from a musician and wakes up one morning wanting to play the piano.* But he said it was more like one of those memories of childhood that comes to you as a fragrance—carried to you on the air, wafting up from the Wound, the little flowers that grow on the trees along Waters in spring.

"A plastic surgeon can give you a new belly button, hon," one of the home care nurses told him; they came once a week to check her work. "Those people can do anything now."

He didn't want a new one, though. The lack of a belly button would uncreate him in God's image—the perfect situation for a man to create his own religion. "Listen to this," her husband said, who was once again able to look at his phone without falling off the edge of the earth. "In 1977, [Garry] Shandling was involved in a car crash in Beverly Hills that left him in critical condition for two days and hospitalized for two weeks with a crushed spleen. While in the hospital, he had a near-death experience and later said, 'I had a vivid near-death experience that involved a voice asking, Do you want to continue living Garry Shandling's life?'"

Then they would say it to each other: Do you want to continue living Garry Shandling's life? In the place where everything was all of a sudden, where we were all together?

As she opened the scissors she heard the sound of Simon and Chloe cutting out construction paper hearts. Her mother had sent away for an educational video about Colors and Shapes when she was little, in which Chloe and her cousin Simon went around the city looking for circles, hearts, triangles, rectangles—in skyscrapers, manholes, flat-iron buildings, stop signs. When they found one, Chloe would take the corresponding shape and lay it on the object, which then *became hers*. It lit up, pinged, became the right size, and allowed her to pick it up. It seemed she needed these things to furnish her house, which she was allowed to have even as an adult woman who wore *Godspell* makeup and huge clown overalls. Exactly the kind of adult I would grow up to be, she thought, carrying my briefcase of forms around the city, to lay one thing on another and make it mine.

Look, there was a diamond.

I'm in a gondola. . . .

She was not sure why she experienced this briefcase so intensely, and watched the special whenever she stayed home from school. The shape-matching was so obviously erotic that it SOMETIMES seemed like Chloe was going to fuck her cousin? Or that they would be married, and live together in the house of hearts. But what was likelier was that they were two halves of the same person: the one who was already there, and the one who was just arriving. Oh—the color and the shape.

Some days, sure, they fought over the Wound. Because he thought of it as Mine and she thought of it as Mine. You put me in charge of it, she said. You can't take a wound back, once you give it. At night she pictured herself pouring honey on it: antibacterial, from alabaster jars, still flowing after two thousand years. The argument, which recurred so often in their marriage, about whether she could have been a caveman doctor. Or William Carlos Williams, passing into his body for as long as it took to find out what it wanted. And coming out *rested*.

A GI surgeon she talked to later was surprised by her hunger to hear about it. "How do you do it?" she asked, cutting into an enormous sirloin. He dissociated from his feeling of the person, he said thoughtfully, and sent all his focus into that square. Even explaining it seemed to make him uneasy; if he thought about it too much, or put it into words, he might not be able to do it again. As he gestured she saw again those heads bent in industry, those hands flashing down a long piano. His family had once burned a piano in winter for warmth; the white keys all went up in a wave of liquid—exactly how she would have described it if she had been there, the flames swiping a glissando from end to end. But if she had been there as it burned, she would have been a surgeon too.

She felt that she knew about this space of focus because she had written poems. Even a line once that seemed to be about it directly: *Hot swords were slicing through the world-knot*. But she was not a surgeon, or a poet anymore. Instead she was in charge of the Wound. At night she saw herself bent over it, long hair hanging over a lyre. Her husband flinging open his robe and saying, "I'm ready." Anne Carson talking about lack, and the edges of words; Lydia Davis invoking purple *without reference to color*. She looked down at his arms, his torso, his pelvis—and why had she never been able to think of his name as Greek, till now.

"How did your wound feel?"

"It felt like a chasm. *[Laughter.]* Can I say that? It felt sort of slippery. I could never tell how deep it was, so that it seemed like it was going all the way through me. It felt like it was always going to open more, and it also seemed like it would never close."

He hesitated. "Um. It felt . . . sometimes I wondered if it was like having a vagina?"

The relief. "It's in. I put that in."

"What I feared most is that I would look down and there would be blood, that I would wake up and there would be blood on the sheet."

"It's there," she said, holding his hand. "It's in."

"That other people would have to see it. That I would be wearing white . . ."

"That's what it's like," she told him. "The big fear is it would happen in church."

So it had gone all the way through them both, the wound. So they had had the same feelings about it. The wind whistling through it, breath, the distance between two people hurtling to close.

Then there was the funniest thing that had ever happened to them in bed, an episode of female priapism.

They had been in bed for hours, in the bullseye of the night. It looked like the beach at Normandy—her foot was over here, his hand was over there. They had entered into some mutual circular breathing of the type that Kenny G practiced. It seemed it would just keep going, but suddenly, "Something . . . is . . . happening . . ." she told him. "I can't . . ." and she made a circle with her thumb and forefinger, like an Italian journalist had done once on Zoom when they were discussing the difficulty of translating sex gestures. "I think I am actually . . . closing . . ." She felt like an old billionaire who was about to die from Viagra. "If it lasts more than four hours, do we go to the hospital?" she asked, lying on her back with her legs against the wall and an icepack wrapped in a towel between them. They couldn't stop laughing, just like that countdown to New Year's—passing into someone's body and coming out solved. So that's what it was? she thought. You could *heal*?

"Do you feel like you still have it?"

"I do, all the time. There's probably five or ten times a day that I reach down and touch it—lift up my shirt and look."

The sizzling light bulb, the bare sheet on the bed, the white robe; and forty-seven days in the desert, she thought, when I was in charge of the Wound.

But when she went to write about what it was like, it was not like that at all. Looking back, it would seem that she loved it. Hadn't she slept at its feet, with her hair bent down? Hadn't she coaxed it? Hadn't she thought of it day and night, hadn't it flown above her? *I felt that it needed to be fed and I didn't know what to feed it*; honey, she almost told him, over and over, every night. A desire for shapes, the diamond, the lick of flame, the heart . . . had she never really thought about flesh before? The two of them together—when she thought she would close, she had been loved so much. And in bed, finally, two hundred days later, how he guided her hand to his scar.

Doppelgänger

Three weeks ago, Anne Carson had been there. Three weeks ago, the grad student, Emiliano, must have greeted Anne Carson the same way he greeted me—by showing her the salmon burn on his temple, to make her feel better about the huge clumsy bandage on her hand. Did he follow Anne Carson, ask to walk her to the hall—but she forgot him? Show up to class in a shirt he had cut open to the chest, telling her he did it last night? Give her a marble and a pin after her reading that said TO HELL WITH HITLER? Talk to her mother and sister, who had actually made it, who rushed to the front row at the very last minute, for a long time afterward as she signed? "Emiliano," her sister said in a baby voice. "Obsessed."

You are asked, even offered money. You go because in memory, your body is removed, and you fly through the people and the place with no pain, and everything happens at once, in the center of a huge water droplet—there you are at the end, printing PATRICIA ANNE on your W-9. But first you must really live it. "They're paging Marvin

Gaye Jr., they're playing 'Fernando,' there's a magazine in the sundries store called SIMPLY JESUS and I just saw the tannest woman I've ever seen in my life," you write from the South Bend airport, where it is raining. Then classrooms, whiteboards, fluorescent lights, faces; the boundaries of people beginning to breathe; Billy in Advanced Poetry telling you, when you ask, that he "would probably be a wolf, because of the speed?"

> "*Say,*" Anne Carson had written,
> "*at the moment in the interminable dinner*
> *when Coetzee basking*
> *icily across from you at the faculty table is all at once*
> *there like a fox in a glare, asking*
> *And what are your interests?*"

So everyone had been to that dinner. It was always going on—that's what interminable was, not boring. You pulled up a chair for a while, at a restaurant called THE JESUS GRILL, and almost ate, and almost drank, the man across the table from you nodding intently as the waitress pronounced the word *lingonberries*—a perfect student in a fruit class, because the world was learning, and it went on and on.

Even Emiliano was there, diagonal. As he called himself, *the remnant*. Anne Carson had described a student who attended Samuel Beckett's Paris lectures: "Most of the students were doing their nails but one of them (Rosie) wrote down everything he said in a small notebook which she was courteous enough to show me." Rosie "wrote down a Proustian location 'between the incandescent body and the damp body' but didn't catch what he said Proust said was between them. She wrote several times the phrase 'integrity of incoherence' and mentioned her sadness that at the end of term he went off thinking himself a bad lecturer. He was not, she felt, bad. Pauses came at wrong places in his talk, she was grateful for them. I wish I'd kept in touch with Rosie."

Did he write down everything Anne Carson said? Know to the minute when he had met her? Keep writing even in the lecture room, where she kicked up a leg on the conference table like it was a piano and she was Liza Minnelli? Keep writing even when her language broke down, and pauses came at wrong places in her talk, and she had to reach in her bra and take another pill? Just weeks ago I had known how to do this, but that was when Anne Carson was there—being shown the basilica, the grotto, the offensive Columbus murals, uncovered only one or two days a year. Being told the secret: that *Amy Coney Barrett stole the purple hand weights from the gym before she left for the Supreme Court.* Staying in the same room: 116. Trying to pull the accessibility toilet off by herself, till hotel maintenance showed up with screwdrivers. Walking and walking toward what seemed the right place, but only ever making it to RADIATION RESEARCH. Raw wind like a—what would she say—crystal beefsteak. Between the incandescent body and the damp, her mother and sister driving toward her through what her mother kept calling a *massive hydrological event*: getting *pounded so hard*, she told everyone later, that *I thought my windows were going to explode.*

Thinking, I probably won't do this again. Thinking, because of the pills, I probably won't remember. Thinking poets should be free, but someone has to teach Greek. But remembering it all, in the huge water droplet. Emiliano asking a question about *going into other bodies while watching basketball*, and was this something you could tell him how to do? Flying in memory through the bodies with no pain—the hamburger burn on my right hand healed—Emiliano, my mother standing off to one side, my sister glowing next to her, pregnant again.

So the world was healthy. It just went on. I stood at the podium where she had stood, looking down at the woman who had called me that, forty years ago, in Indiana. Three weeks ago Anne Carson shouted MAKE THE STAGE BLACKER! Anne Carson said, deadpan, "I'm not funny." Anne Carson read new work about someone named Anne Carson—Anne Patricia, actually. It was, everyone agreed, more of a performance piece, and really very moving in the end.

The Scrapers

"I'm Belgian!" my husband cried, delighted. He recrossed his legs in what I could tell he thought was a "Belgian way." I knew what this meant: It meant his love of french fries would be elevated above mine for all time.

"This is why you can't grind," I told him. I had once tried to teach a Belgian man to grind at a party, but his body wasn't capable of it. In place of hips he seemed to have a filing cabinet. So too my husband, who had refused to even waltz at our wedding. He considered my dancing too . . . too . . .

"French Canadian," he had exclaimed in triumph, when my Ancestry Dot Com results had come in, which revealed that I had been descended from seventeenth-century whores.

"What else?" I asked, as he leaped up from the couch and returned in a more tailored pair of pants. "It says," he read modestly, "that I have the sprinter gene. It says I sneeze twice in the sunlight. . . . It says I have unusually beautiful eyes that cause everyone to trust me."

I took the phone from him. It actually did say that. "Unibrow," I read out loud. "Bald."

The test told you whether you had cilantro aversion, or asparagus metabolite detection, or alcohol flush. "God, it would be so fun to be doing this drunk," we agreed, but we did not get drunk anymore. Instead, we paid twenty more dollars so that we could see mine; these more granular results had not been available when I spit into the tube five years ago.

"Beta carotene deficient," I read sadly. "Omega-3 deficient, vitamin D deficient. Heart recovers at a lower than average rate. Lactose intolerant."

My husband was laughing. "Oh, here's a good one," I said bravely. "Average size newborn."

"Let me see about your eyes," he said. I had been avoiding that part. "Iris patterns: furrows, crypts, and rings. Furrows are a sign of impulsiveness."

"No unibrow," I said, almost crying. Belgians were so cruel. In high school, he had once given a friend a nickname; the nickname was Anal Dave.

"You might pass on the red-hair trait to children," he said, frowning, but we had never had any of those. Examining my VO_2 max, he said, "Your body does not appear to use oxygen at all."

"It should tell us whether we can dance," I said, rising from the couch to see whether I could still grind. The last time we had gotten drunk together, I had tried to teach him in the bathroom, pressing him to my hips, putting one hand on either side of his filing cabinet while blasting late-nineties hip-hop. "Look at me in the mirror," I commanded, and he looked into my eyes and trusted me, despite furrows, crypts, and deep dark rings. For a moment we were carrying each other over the threshold and it was once more the night of the wedding. "Ladies and gentlemen . . . the bride . . . the groom . . ." No children, despite the presence I felt now, of a tall, easy son who took things down from shelves for me. Seventeen years old, warm smell of waffles on weekends, and why was he running so swiftly away?

Black ice and a reception in the little school hall, and firelight dancing on our faces. It was the sort of wedding beasts would have, I was always happy to remember. We were like something out of winter folklore, both the children and the wolves simultaneously, staring at ourselves with orange eyes from the dark, poised to pounce and grapple and roll, tearing a private language from the tender place in our throats. Tall hills piled above us and Lil Jon playing; snow silently blanketing the incline; the crack of cubes in glasses and below all, the river running.

I love taking my baby to the mountains *shit*, the Mailman said, posing in front of a toxic heap of slag along River Road—the same one, possibly, that had been visible from the front rectory window. Thems nice little mountains you better leave them alone. My brother PJ had sent us another Mailman video; we were obsessed. The Mailman was white and had grills and lived near the local graveyard and referred to everyone as lil stank-stank. One could accuse him of the most complete act of cultural appropriation the world had ever known, but one look at him and that framework fled your mind entirely.

Thirty seconds of his voice, surprisingly resonant in the lower registers, and you entered a new reality: Ohio, Cincinnati, West Side, Price Hill, our old address.

A former Scraper, for sure, Daniel said. He was the authority. His childhood had been different from mine, as perhaps the childhoods of boys must be. Squirrels had been blown up by firecrackers. Dumpster fires had been set. Mountain Dews stolen from convenience stores. We were lucky he had not joined the child gang called the Scrapers, who didn't go to school, and threatened, rather poetically, to scrape people. They roamed around all day and threw rocks at cars. Once they broke into school and bit a teacher on the leg.

I was howling—how had I not known about the Scrapers? This was an existence that I was suddenly, helplessly able to imagine. Rovings in creeks, child marriages in the woods, initiation rites. Swipes of mud under the eyes and raccoon tails tied around the waist—Lost Boys, who slept not in houses but in hollow trees, in skin-to-skin contact with the stars. Who were they, where were their parents, what Bible were they sworn in on? Careful, I cautioned myself. One sign that your actual life was over was a fresh interest in genealogy; shapes crowding around you, the tall, nonexistent son striding away in his basketball shorts, a coupon for free coneys in his pocket, delinquent from the duty of ever being born.

"All men are my sons!" my mother had screamed once. Lately, a little loosened—sweet again, like a child—she had been telling secrets. That my grandfather Pierce, a Mailman, wasn't drafted into WWII because he had "too few teeth," for instance. That sounded just like the floating toe thing, but she swore: 4-F, too few teeth. She had told me about hidden pregnancies and Bluebeard's wives and second cousins who were getting blow jobs on Craigslist, "ONLY receiving, never giving." She had told me about BLASIUS, a great-great-uncle who had run a mutual aid society down in Over-the-Rhine, which shuttered after it detonated the ass of an Italian with some sort of electrified paddle during an initiation rite. He had come there for aid, and we had blown up his ass and given him lockjaw. That's very, very us, I said sadly. Lil stank-stanks. Later BLASIUS had opened a speakeasy down on the river, a warren of candlelit hidey-holes during Prohibition. At once I saw the firelight on familiar faces, me and Daniel and Mary and PJ slipping down through the mud and toward the music. Wait wait wait, I told her, hold up. You're telling me that Banjo Town was real?

But she didn't remember entering that dream with us, crossing the railroad tracks, seeing the shanties; all of it playing out in the bourbon-brown light. The bridge to Kentucky was currently on fire; a scrape job, very possibly, as Daniel speculated. What if you had gotten stuck there? my husband asked, watching one of the small-town episodes of *The X-Files* where the citizens are all in a blood-drinking cult. What if you had married a townie? I almost did, I said thoughtfully, but it was hard to tell how close, how really close I had come. Heidi and I didn't know what we were doing, I could now cheerfully admit. In one version we had kind of made me a Juggalo; encountering a high school acquaintance at the First Watch, I had fist-bumped her and gone *Whoop whoop*. But no, stolen valor, that didn't ring true. I belonged to a different child gang, stripped to the waist, scampering through brambles behind the Holy Grail.

How had I been carried to a place of safety? Oh God, I could see the graveyard where the Mailman lived, driving past it in the white

Thunderbird with my boyfriend after eating a glamorous chicken tender dinner. His lower lip fat with chaw. Mountain Dew in the cup holder. It was impossible to tell how many teeth the Mailman had: a thousand. He appeared in his videos with his mail hat turned sideways and a tall unopened letter in his shirt pocket. From the "thems" I could conclude he must be around PJ's age. Something had gone askew with that generation. Lil stank ole booty I love y'all, said the Mailman, swiping an animal paw at the camera. His whole mouth a single diamond. Only people in like a twenty-mile radius can truly understand this, agreed my brothers with a bone-deep weariness, and even I had to admit that stank-stank, in its way, was a pronoun that applied with benediction to all.

Another secret let slip was the information that my grandmother was a high school dropout. I admit this did surprise me. She was so classy, a freshly rolled pageboy, standing in an avenue of trees on her wedding day. Yet she, too, was running away from her family in that photo, just as I had done. She had been forced to leave school at sixteen to care for her mother, an imaginary invalid whose children (future Scrapers) were always trying to jump off the roof. It was that caretaking, my mother told me, and her brother Ed going missing in the war, that had led to her madness, and then she fled those duties forever, delivered by her Mailman. Even to look at the lace on her dress, my mother said, it was clear she came from wealth: a stitched swanskin without a single tear. She thought her life was going to be different, as we all did. Instead she woke every morning at a strange address, the flow of picture postcards she should have been receiving diverted in a stream all around her.

I was the sole receptacle for this legend. My mother never told it to the other children, but to me, she had spoken a hundred times of that madness and her subsequent decision not to be mad. It was this that fascinated me, could not be squared. My grandmother as I knew her had been eminently sane, stirring a calm whirlpool into her eternal cup of coffee, sitting across from me in the booth at Price Hill Chili. After her Mailman passed away she had gone back to school and become a nurse, who talked of the human body at the dinner table; so had I met her and thought of her still. Again and again I tried to pin down this nebulous period. When was she mad? When did she talk to herself so that you had to walk six feet ahead of her in the street, pretending not to know her as you pretended not to know our clouds? When, and how, did she *go not mad*? Was it something any person might be able to decide?

Mail was the family business; everyone had gone out of it but me. Someone in each generation had to be taught the route. This one, my own ancestral Mailman had said thoughtfully, cupping my clinically large occipital lobe, is different. Toothless, drooling, rolling wherever I wanted to go; not average size as I had been promised, but enormous. She will do something, he said. Maybe he only meant: Carry this letter, it holds what we know, and whistle past the graveyard to deliver it. If hell existed—and we had glimpsed it—it was the Lost Mail Room, where things of this world were misdelivered.

I dream of a life back in town. Not past, but a future, or parallel. The war that was coming would be between the Scrapers—who survived, who scratched their own existence out of the dirt—and the rest. In that war you will need more teeth, for your hunger, than the human mouth can hold. But we steal our beef jerky from convenience stores, we are the Scrapers. Listen to me, lil stank-stank, we'll make it. Burn bridges, crawl through windows. Bite that teacher on the leg.

Beginning Metals

In the class, I melted metal. In the beginning, I could not tell what was supposed to be interesting about it. You formed it, and you forged it. You hammered, sawed, textured; polished it against the wheel and your eyes. There was a right way to do things, and then there was my discovery: You could hold the flame steady and not take it away; you could let go and let it happen to you.

The teacher, infinitely patient, did not understand. She would come over and say, Still melting? I advocated for my activity. It was teaching me what the metal was thinking, I said. What it was about to do. It began to shimmer and got a red look. The whole air around you turned to mirage. You would think inexplicably of *The Lord of the Rings*, and that Gary Larson panel about amoeba porno, and there, long lances of wire raced back along themselves, a brief heap of auto parts, a pile of crumb topping, the color orange was trying to go back to its original body, and then the whole thing flew into itself, it melted.

Everyone else, over the last few years, had become obsessed with pottery, but I don't give a fuck about a cup, I said. And I didn't care about baking my own bread either. It's like I was on strike against the Last Supper. I was with the silver, on the Judas side. I have twenty years of this, I told the teacher, indicating my bag of scrap. A lifetime's worth. I melted.

I was the class incompetent. I haven't been in a classroom since high school—except teaching, I did not say—but everything I had been in those days flashed upon me. I was still what I was: a fact-Chihuahua, yelping answers as if someone were hitting me with a reflex hammer. I had even made an enemy, by yelling TORCH! at one girl as she was using the torch. I thought I still heard the hiss of breath, when she laid it down. My essential self chased me, always on my heels. I am going to come back as a *calm* person, I told myself, but that was a risk: What if I returned as my own husband, and had to go looking for a new kind of me. Never free.

At nine o'clock he would pull up and wait. He would turn on the dome light and ask to see what I had done, as he used to come home from the paper and ask to see the poem, and we would drive over bridges into the black east. My breath came short and sharp, as if I had metal-fume fever. I could still feel the click of the starter under my hand. Once we saw green lightning on the way home, like the whole thing, as my teacher would tell me, were *about to go*. We cried out together, Oh! Then: Were we the only people in the world who saw that, though why should that be true, more than any other lightning. Do you think we were the only ones in the world.

I melted. My riches were an embarrassment. All that silver. Twenty years. Cherry red. Dull red. Rosy pink. You're painting with the flame. The metal is alive. It has a skin on it, shining. Let it spin for thirty seconds. You are the sun, or something else. Don't take away the heat too soon. Eternal interest, to make organic forms. You might have been something else. Will be something else next time. "It looks like cum," I confessed to the teacher, showing her my creation. But, "Everything I make looks like that at some point," she said.

At the last moment, you will see the metal *relax*, the teacher told us, and showed her own shoulders going down.

That's the Blue Cone of Nothingness, she said to me. Stay out of the Blue Cone of Nothingness.

How do you know when to stop? I asked, and she danced in a half circle away. That's a life lesson.

In one corner of the classroom, the tumbler was always going, like the earth. It made things bright, little BBs in a wash of soap. Kim had to feed it things, like Pnin and the washing machine. You could turn your back and she was sneaking in something she bought at Claire's in 1999. Not turquoise, Kim! you would cry to her. She shrugged her shoulders. You turned your back. The tumbler was hungry. The turquoise went in.

"I love Social Crafting," declared Lori, her chest expanded to its modest limit. She wore a lot of crisp wind-filled shirts, like a sailboat. She had to leave right at nine so she could be home to watch *The Golden Bachelor*. Because of the milieu, it was possible to picture him as actual gold. Is he hot? I asked, and my enemy hooted, then dropped her dendritic limestone again. "Have we met before?" Lori had asked in the first class. "I'm a writer," I said, but she shook her head, waved away my entire profession. Eventually my enemy figured it out. I was famous to them, but not as myself—as a renowned local acupuncturist.

I'm disappointed in him, Lori said of the Golden Bachelor. I think he went with the money.

My enemy came in late, with a can of Liquid Death in her hand.

The hammering, the drilling, the trapped refrain.

We weren't real enemies, really, we just didn't know each other's names. So there was daylight between us, that was this not knowing, the solder wouldn't run. Still, to have an enemy felt both primal and European, like one of those psychological novels where women had to hang each other's dogs back and forth for eternity, or show up at each other's birthday parties with bare bleeding feet. Only when she revealed that she was a volleyball coach did I understand that it was *butch tension*.

Was this like when Sheila Heti briefly became a hairdresser? Or when Kurt Cobain wanted to run a 7-Eleven? Or when my sister tried to be on *Storage Wars* instead of standing in a side chapel and singing? It was exhausting to be bound to your actual duty, what you were good at. I examined my latest blob, which looked like either a radish or the Sacred Heart. Would it be like that sad thing where we all had to pretend to care about Sylvia Plath's drawings of shoes? But I had thought, I had really thought, Maybe I won't have to write poems anymore. You could start a business, my husband reflected, and call it Oh You Blob Ring Fool.

At the garden show, Nathalie sold a copper plant accessory for eight dollars. Maybe I can quit my job, she said. What's your job? I asked. I'm a scientist, Nathalie said very softly. Doesn't it need you, though? I asked her. Science? But no, she had come to the end of her field, as I had come to mine. Why was I making refrains, when they brought us less close to reality? I could do this, and not look for the moment when the words would begin to slip their skins like plums or tomatoes—or people. Even Mallory, she had quit her job placing pomegranate seeds one by one with tweezers, and had taken up a post making birthday cakes at Costco.

Kathy would glance up at you with a look of love, or else a look of not being able to hear you that well. She was out one week—not COVID, she had tested twice—and returned with bright red eyes and a wild, joyful personality. Maybe it was the child personality, which had flashed out of my grandmother and was now flashing out of my mother. Suddenly very funny, flinging her arms up in pantomime. Coughing so hard that she rolled off the couch and burst both of the ice packs she had on her knees. "I'll tell you what's in them . . . *goo*."

I melted. I could put a spleen back in the human body. Little puddles, drops of overflow. Something began to spin, the sun was coming out. Creatures and plants were raised upon the earth. "Are they beautiful?" someone asked Nathalie, about plankton under a microscope. "They *are* beautiful," she said, after a hesitation, and began to describe them with her hands. "Some are little urchins with tons of spikes. Others are amoeba-type beasts . . ." and she drew a long horn coming out of her forehead. I should have asked her about the rain of shrimps, I realized, though I did not think of it, far from the plague and the fall.

At work they used to call me MacGyver, Kathy said, and I believed her. The new joyful personality was still intact. Imitating a survivalist she knew, she yelled, "When shit goes down, you'll WISH you had my can of tuna!" No, when shit went down, you'll wish you had a MacGyver, who, at the hospital, back in the day, was famous for "always making something out of something else." It sounded alarming in practice, but perhaps those survivalist days had already come. Imagine her on a house visit, fluxing the seam of my husband, imagine what she might have done with the Wound!

Have you done your casting yet? we kept asking each other, like, Have you gotten your dress for the dance? What you were going to cast seemed very personal somehow, like you had only one shot at it. Mallory had a chickpea, because she was vegan. Someone else had done an acorn, which was a favorite choice because of the distinct cross-hatching on the cap, and because to wear an acorn around your neck seemed so rich, like you had everything you needed for the winter. My enemy had a long thin wishbone. She wanted to feel the silver flash down into it on the instant, like a day spent reading about the Lichtenberg figures on Wikipedia compressed into a single moment. I had chosen the little brain in the man suit, Krang, who was always crying in a horrible voice, MY BODY! I had an action figure of him that I kept on my desk. I didn't want anyone to watch me do it. I just wanted to have him suddenly, in my hand.

The night it came to do my casting I chopped mud for two and a half hours. You had to get all the lumps out before you started—never tell me that! I would pack the cylinder, push the brain in, and realize it was wrong somehow—I had forgotten to put proper air holes, or the clay wasn't dense enough, or he was positioned in such a way that the sprue of metal would spew out of his mouth. It was like designing a man—this one won't live, I would understand, as I would pry apart the cylinder and examine the impression. Two of the child women had never even heard of the Teenage Mutant Ninja Turtles so I had to do the voice for them over and over: TURTLES! MY BODY!

Girl you crazy, Kim said over my shoulder, in an intimate tone, having just fed a huge ammonite pendant to the tumbler. Kim, what do you do for a living? I asked her, brushing my high and tight off my forehead with the back of my wrist. Radio DJ, she told me, low, on Magic 103.

In the corner, my enemy was doing water casting into a huge metal pail. I got a big one! she cried, like a pearl diver, reaching elbow-deep down in the water.

I'm a scientist, I could hear from Nathalie's corner, an *ocean* scientist.

I could have cried with laughter. It was clear I was never going to stop chopping the clay. The other students who had done castings, their pieces had been full of pits, because they hadn't been "as . . . careful about it as you are being," said the teacher, carefully. I had been writing about suicide all morning—a friend's, not mine. March 2020. My fingertips were stained a deep earth brown. I buried my object over and over, dusted with baby powder. I'm making all the mistakes so you don't have to, I would apologize, every time someone came to check my progress. "I have a pastry tool you could use for that," MacGyver said kindly, from across the table. I saw my friend standing then next to one of her cakes. My fingertips went searching among the cool crumbs—flour, sugar, butter.

After you've done it three or four times you'll want to stop and add a little fresh metal, said the teacher, as she demonstrated. It's like an eclipse, she said, aiming the flame at the crucible. You want to look but not look. But I looked, we all did. A children's book I could never find again, about a boy who digs up, in his backyard, a ball of entirely new color. I thought I saw it then: that white indigo vaporous peach. As it began to go it was like crowds, or birds wheeling up. When you think it's ready, wait sixty more seconds, she said. We watched. Something vulnerable in the back and shoulders of someone who had been on the production line. She had forgotten to tie her hair back; it flowed forward. Silver threads running through, and mine. She held the flame at the lip, as the color gathered, ready to fall. You have to tell yourself you're going to do it, she said, bracing herself, and then actually . . . she poured. We gathered around to see.

Each time you did it you would fail. Each time you would know a little more.

No, you're perfect, my enemy said over my shoulder. She was exactly six feet tall.

We shook our heads. No, this one wouldn't make it. So melt again.

The walls breathing in and out. The spinning skin. The world a little granule. Then the green flash.

Then suddenly, like a cure, everyone was better. You could see their ideas in the air, you could stand up and walk through them like warm Caribbean currents. "I just love it," you would often hear someone saying to herself, "don't you just love it?" It was no longer all-girls' school, even, for there was now a big bouncing boy named Kaleb, who wore semi-ironic duck-hunting shirts and whose energy pitched us all to the point of hysteria. "Thursdays are all about *metal* for me," he said, flinging his curls off his face. He was working sculpturally;

none of us had done that before. Sudden cavewoman abashment—were we little basket weavers, while he would build bridges? Stirring porridge, while he set gems in the bowl of the spoon? It didn't matter. He was our son, or the other way around, the spoon flew into all our mouths like an airplane.

Security guards surrounded us. The vice president was being unloaded into the Civic Center across the street. *You think you just fell out of a coconut tree?* But we didn't care, we were bent over our work. We hadn't looked up for three hours. *You exist in the context of all in which you live and what came before you.* Kaleb was polishing his spoon, either for art or for someone to eat with. Terri was considering a rhodochrosite and Mary was setting a coin pearl. Laura was, for unknown reasons, making a bezel for a small black replica of her dog's nose. This was wonderful. She never, in conversation, betrayed the slightest suspicion that this might be funny, so it wasn't, the nose became real. Kathy was braiding six strands of wire; she was trying to be more creative. Emily was setting a malachite into the cover of a leather journal. And I—I was making calyxes, oysters, islets of Langerhans. Little petals of fire, falling. I was putting them back on the rose.

We had moved from the islands back downtown, to a second-story unit above a pizza restaurant. There was someone living on the roof, strange to report—up in the sky where we were, his camouflage failed to hide him. He had the new weedy haircut that had spread around the neighborhood, courtesy of a woman called the Hair Witch. Only a thin pane of glass separated us, he could see everything I was doing, but I refused to give up that fine clear gold through the window, which used to be my reading light.

On one bookshelf we had lovingly placed the Flaws. This was a secular nativity scene I had given my husband one year for Christmas. The wise men were three obelisks of ocean jasper. Their frankincense and myrrh was a cube of pyrite, and the baby, nestled in a milk-glass salt cellar, was a shiva lingam stone. My husband pronounced it the best gift he had ever received. He arranged it all on a tray table to contemplate, then reclined his La-Z-Boy in perfect satisfaction and kicked the whole thing high in the air. I overheard it in the bathroom: Don't tell her! my husband wailed to his mother, Don't tell her! I saw myself in the mirror then, what I was. Everything broken in some small way or other; we spent the night, the three of us, putting it back together with glue. Joseph was the most grievously injured, his blue robe cracked from head to toe, but my husband bent over him, a surgeon, not breathing, and then held him up whole on the tip of one finger, sealed.

Leaned up against the window was my big bag of silver, which did not seem to diminish. I knew no one would ever steal it; it was my life. After a while I put the aumônière there as well. I imagined someone at a pawnshop, emptying stars onto black velvet. And here's an Ocean Picture Stone. And here's a Pecos Diamond. Here's the one she calls the Scar. When I held something small in the palm of my hand, I always thought, Poor little thing, you're home now. It's all right, I've got you, I would say to the earth in miniature.

Tall bulbs of crystal. Great eyes like glass. My fear, as a child cradling my identification guide, that we would somehow *run out of stones*. They have come all this way to us, I said, with weird passion. They have been put into our care. I knew where there was a rutile and where there was a rainbow and where there was a flake like manna of mica, falling. I had put them in my mouth. I would never break one, though everyone did eventually. They were like bodies to me. I knew what they could take. Are you good with your hands, the teacher asked, and I laughed, though I had closed the Wound, though there was still some tenderness between my fingers that was like the pinching of snapdragons.

MacGyver was a Wound Specialist, she told us at lunch over her Aztec bowl. She had simply gotten interested in it. "I'm all in," she might have said, as she said when she bought her ring-bending machine or her dapping set or her kiln; "I'm really doing it." If she pricked her own finger she nearly fainted, but other people were another story—there was a shining tool, a perfect stitch, for everything that could happen to you. I don't like laparoscopic surgery, she said, shaking her head; I don't think the doctors can really *see*. She knew all about belly button reconstruction and she told us about new technology—a black sponge that slowly drew you together again.

What I think now is: People are amazing. It was true, people were capable of the most unbelievable measurements. People made springs and closures and hinges. They multiplied by pi to find the diameter. They cut seats for sapphires smaller than glints. The terrifying aspect was not that it was impossible, it was that you started to see how they could do it. Was everything this way? Could I have learned Greek?

In class I wore one of the teacher's necklaces, which had never been fitted to a human body. Would you wear it for an hour? she asked, and it was like God asking you to keep watch in the garden. I bowed my head and Kathy and Terri fastened it around my neck, in the grave and laughing role of ceremonial attendants. The links lay perfectly, even as I sawed, measured, hummed. I thought it was the necklace called Music, which had been displayed in the show next to mine. MUSIC? she said, aghast—making her funniest face, her hater face. You didn't call it that? I faltered. Oh no, another mistake, just like the Kevin Carlos Williams thing. I would never call it that, she said. The name of it is Expansion.

Expansion fell in light orbit around my neck. It needed no adjustment whatsoever.

Kaleb hung his spoon on the wall, where it turned a kind of honey color.

I haven't seen anything beautiful for 136 days because of the war.

I was setting a pale yellow fossil coral cabochon, with what looked like two slices of lemon floating in it. I was setting a starry green prasiolite, and a slab of larimar like the ocean in matrix. Now, you'll want to put the loops here, the teacher cautioned, where they will be most beautiful. I didn't tell you, but what you are attempting is quite difficult. Well, I could do it this way, I said, trying the ocean vertically. The teacher said in her wonderful voice, Ugly. I know! I said. Why is it so ugly? Because it was not the way the soul sat in it—it went like that, it waved. I supposed these were basic principles of design, but why think about it that way when you could just say in the wonderful voice, Ugly. Looking at any wrong thing.

Sometimes the teacher would flash into quick beauty like a metal. This must have been true of the rest of us too. Bent over, on the ultimate production line: people making things. But you are learning, Terri, I said in earnest, when one of the joins in her copper form failed. We weren't adding to lostness or failure, we were adding to learning. Think of all the high polish lost down garbage disposals or in the sea. My mother's wedding ring had disappeared on a hayride, which seemed symbolic. I could make her another one, I thought. Could make her another husband. Could be born again.

When you came out of class it was like you had—been born again, that is. Limbs wavy, in a kind of open, rubbery sleepwalk, you stopped at the desk of Tyriq, King of the Women. One by one, in their childlike overalls and with their toolboxes, the women waited their turn to show Tyriq what they had done. Little cups and saucers, brass sculptures, realistic hog ceramics—all had to pass under his level gaze. All the feeling you were trying to put into the clay or metal would spill toward him, as it must spill toward the users of any real object. Tyriq's voice created his face; you never saw him without a mask. He remained the beholder, the pair of hands, the great person for whom things were made.

So use was what made something real. Warm skin was the surface we polished and polished toward. It was not like poetry at all, or else it was—it is like your words are washing me, a student once said after a reading. It was like it ended a dozen times before it did, said another. Gold Heidi, onstage, made an encompassing gesture and spoke of the *penumbra*: the idea that the law held some people not in the center of protection but in its glow. But I was subject to a different law here, and I could make it: amulets, worry beads, coins free of any country. I could marry people more properly than my father, tie a knot that would last for a thousand years.

Then I was rising in the air. Then I was upside down, mining opals in Australia. The teacher accompanied me to the Sensory Room and sat me there in the dark, next to the light-up panels and the tactile tree, until the genius of headaches subsided. I was a fleck, a flashing lance, a rainbow. Some quartzes have bubbles of water in them, fresh, that still move. My whole skin racing as if everything were art, as if it were not just ordinary life but art that was trying to surface in me. My father, making the turn onto the beach access road, telling me it might be the tides—the tug and pull of that huge silver body, which some people must feel more than others.

But I was at the sea again, with my family. Not getting sucked in. My nephews dug clams, which appeared to breathe near the creamy gray hinge. I had one whose breath and sweet inner cushion had been entirely replaced by crystals. I could set one. I had whelks and ammonites and petrified bogwood in mille-feuille layers. I had a fairy stone that looked like Saturn; I had the stone from Scotland that I called the Exchange; I had dendritic agates, white and fogged, with pictures like hospital windows. Make something for me, my mother said—turning seventy at the stroke of midnight. I like jasper. There is one, I told her, that looks like a landscape out west, there is Biggs and Blue Mountain and Gary Green. I offered her all of it, vast terrain, the Grand Canyon when we were little.

We had been at the birth of the world together: a long drive on Route One the morning after a cousin's wedding, when I was hungover and still slightly high; I dipped in and out of sleep as she drove, and every so often would wake to some new extraterrestrial landscape: the moon, Venus, Mars, as if we were traveling all the way out together, in ripples. I would wake, exclaim at the slopes out the window, and then slip back into most heavenly, cared-for sleep. Possibly the flying was meant to feel that way: an aerial view, freedom, trust in some heavenly grip. No one had ever seen the West the way we did that morning. She might not remember, but I could frame that for her too.

I was cupping her face as I sometimes did, so that it shone out of its setting. You simply surround them, I said to her. You surround them and they are safe. I hardly know how it works either, but it does. Silver is so soft, every scar you put in you have to take out—but ours, in the beach light, faded to almost nothing.

I showed them the lemon slices, an impossible color on me. My niece Angel tried the necklace on, unfinished, and touched the stone like a talisman, smiling. The thing in the world, whatever it was, worked. It swung from her neck in fresh slices. She will have the privilege of losing it, I thought, on a hayride, in the ocean. It is her life, I kept saying to whoever would listen, This is her one life, let her live it. She had read to me, haltingly, the dozen oysters of Walter Benjamin. She squeezed the rind between her fingers and drank a raw one now.

We stood at the edge of the freezing sea. She reached down to scoop, with her rigid hand, those mobile pearls. Laughing out loud, with her bright teeth, whenever a wall of water hit her. Her other hand she had snuck into mine. She did not touch people, this had never happened before. I was missing, it did not matter, the last lesson on Clasps.

And was I responsible for the *pattern*, the circles, the overlap, the repetition? "I'm retiring," my doctor told me at my last appointment. "You know, I've been doing this for thirty years, and I want to have more time for my metalsmithing." No, I thought, it couldn't be. "Your teacher?" I asked. And it was.

The other little girls drifted out to me. The waves tumbled us higher and higher. I screamed every time, to show them it was all right, that I was there and we would not go under. The one life swung lightly around my niece's neck. I was holding more hands than I had. Everything was crisscrossing, was in the same place, we were all just together, were together.

Try to make a ring whose seam I cannot find.

And I have eyes like a hawk, said the teacher.

The Art of Biography

In the birthplace of the heteronym, the interest was in biography. Maria thought she could write a biography of an object—as a break, perhaps, from the book she had been writing for the past fifteen years, about flattery in Shakespeare. Faces were destiny. She looked like she came from the sixteenth century, like she ought to be wearing a little jerkin. You could write about the black cock, Teresa suggested. There was a national story about black cocks that no one quite knew the rights of. The circle of scholars gathered closer, taking turns to reconstruct. It involved a false accusation against a Galician, who, as he was being sentenced to death, yelled to a roast chicken in the middle of the table, "If I am innocent! That cock will sing!" And it did sing, just as they dropped him—however, just to be safe, the Portuguese had also tied the knot in his noose wrong. The black cocks, as a decoration, were everywhere, to remind people to be fair to Galicians. You *should* write a biography of that, I said. It might go faster than the Shakespeare one. Certainly it would go faster than the biography someone was writing about dunes, for the pile would grow higher, and they would always change.

And I was there because allegedly I had written a biography—of who or what, I had no idea. I was in a vulnerable state. As always, for forty-eight hours after switching time zones, I experienced identifiable human emotions. Knew when I was hungry, knew when I was thirsty, where normally I could not name any passing current. Also, Teresa had come. Had been caught, when Maria touched her sleeve to introduce us. She did not usually leave her house—when she did, someone would give her a puppy, or try to carry her off in a taxi. That's how it was for me too, and possibly how it was for all poets, as you could see from reading about them. For instance, I had broken my toe the night before by dropping a Lady Secret on it. Oh no, Teresa and I thought, as we dragged across the room toward each other, it happened to us and for the same reasons; there was a deep desire in things to be *told*.

In one corner the Beatles biographer typed furiously. Or of a coffee cup, someone else went on, as the rest of us sat drinking our espressos. Teresa was on the floor, I didn't want her on the floor, with everything inside me I was lifting her up. She often had to order another, she said, because a duck would steal across the lawn of the Gulbenkian and drink hers in a single sip. She would go back up to the snack bar and the barista would say, "Let me guess, a duck?" No word on whether they drank everyone's espresso, or just hers. "We'll have to workshop that," she said, shaking her head, when I suggested she write a poem called "Thirst."

For she had given it up, she had given up poetry—or was keeping it secret, as I was. "And everyone knew this notebook existed?" I asked after the Sylvia Plath session. I had been freaking out quietly during the talk, squiveling in my seat, chafing against invisible restraints, as I always did when academics talked about poets—something about it seemed to make them dead. But yes, everyone knew it but me. A mad girlfriend of Ted's had stolen it; you had to envy him the certainty of his type. We have dreams of its extreme recovery—black catsuits, night walks along a ridgepole, and at the end of everything, jewels in the hand, last entries, the sure knowledge of why she had done it. Biography was gossip; I could have been in the stream of it all along.

But I could not read them; they seemed to make us dead, and to fail to understand the swell under the feet, the thing that sparked it. Why that, why then? Whom did she love, who was the Master? Why those years? people were always asking about Emily Dickinson, but it was the war—and every day, in the paper, and in the air, and over the tea table, came *the postponeless Creature*. Why guns, and black crape, and cages, and why did she write fewer poems in 1866? Not because she was too overcome. Because she would not be that overcome again. As I had neglected to write, in any book about her.

"Butterfly come be my little . . . BUUUUURD," piped the fado singer through the hotel halls.

But the number struck me, and the number within the number. Had all that happened in four years? It was like the sight of the British in the summer of 2021, wearing Bo Peep dresses and looking like they had been through a war. The Portuguese were a little pale, they exclaimed over my bare shoulders in my hideous art-teacher smock, they would not truly come alive, they said, until the sun shone on them in July. In the lectures, coughs came scattered across the rows.

Maria cleared her throat; the sickness had hit her hard—she had lost her scholar's memory, been unable to read, and had the same trouble retrieving. The first two letters of a name would come, we agreed, but then the rest would be wrong. Treacherous, when your subject was flattery. You might find yourself in the wrong clown, turning cartwheels for an incorrect Henry.

For some reason I could not seem to escape the conference, to cross the enchanted perimeter into the city; there was something in the green room, and in the mazelike gardens on the property, where shadow cats went slipping and the teens wrapped each other like vines. A national story was being built, in that tightening circle of scholars; all of us were required, even me and the dune guy. I left and came back, left and came back, past the jugglers who threw clubs in the crosswalks, high into the squint of the air. The cure for jet lag was to go walking with your bare feet in the grass—Teresa brightened, for she had grown up in the country—but no, I said, no one could ever see that toe. Two rubies reached out to me from her left hand; I could set them. And . . . did she know there was a kind called the *record-keeper?* She was a poet, I must remember to tell her.

Who was it? They had emailed me about it, probably, but if you emailed me now it went into a place called Eternity. I counted my obsessions off on my fingers. Someone had written about Carmen Miranda—now there was an idea. The simultaneous translation kept breaking down during that one; the crowd in the auditorium would roar, so I knew a joke had come, but always missed it. What was clear was that he worshipped her, and her green-apple eyes, and her lips parted for a kiss in one of the anecdotes. If she had put the date on her final autograph, he said heavily, and I saw bananas and her black hair tumbling down, we would know that was the last person to ever see Carmen Miranda alive. This was the burden the biographer carried; there was always some encounter that could not make it into record, but was tucked with the handkerchief next to the heart. The *heart?* What was I saying? But I was still in the forty-eight hours.

My jacket was full of fruit. I also had a bag of macadamias, but I kept them hidden out of courtesy for Teresa, who was afraid of nuts. Poets were the same everywhere, I smiled, in Amherst, in Yeats's cold-water flat, in Lisboa. I took out my freckled pear and ate it, but I had chosen poorly from the pyramid at the corner store. You couldn't go by color, Teresa explained, and then we were looking at each other too much for a moment, it had to be tender near the stem. What is the scent in Lisbon? I kept asking, everywhere and nowhere, like chamomile or jasmine—but not even the biographer of the existentialists could identify it, and Teresa had not been able to smell anything for a month.

The time was approaching. Who in my life had I thought most about? All would be revealed during my hour, when the huge face of my subject would be projected behind me. Huge faces on projectors were a dangerous game. I began the Iris Murdoch session wondering why everyone was in love with Iris Murdoch. At the end of it I was in love with Iris Murdoch. Her biography, full of slits and blacked-out pages, had been written by two women simultaneously, a kind of marriage; the whole crowd was intrigued. Her bangs cut with a machete, her caveman eyes full of desire. Actually, hadn't I written about her too, or made notes? In *The Sea, the Sea* . . . a dog tooth truly seen . . .

If even a dog's tooth is truly worshipped it glows with light. The venerated object is endowed with power, that is the simple sense of the ontological proof. And if there is art enough a lie can enlighten us as well as the truth. What is the truth anyway, that truth? As we know ourselves we are fake objects, fakes, bundles of illusions. Can you determine exactly what you felt or thought or did?

Portuguese women all had to be gay because the men were preoccupied with football. During the final panel, the luminous male interviewer, seemingly polished with sugar, was said to be checking the score. Afterward, we went to a restaurant—Teresa parting ways to walk her great animal—me and Maria and Nuno, who had hair like a wolfman. They turned off the game after we were seated and Nuno became agitated. "WHERE IS MY GAME?" I shouted, to make clear that the passion was mine. "I need my game!" The waiters hurried over, relieved. Then all of us were happy, the waiters and Nuno watching, and Maria and I tormenting him with suggestions that the field should be smaller.

The night was beginning to feel like the dreams I would have later: the tree of blossoms on a lake, two flowers bending down and down until with a burst of agony they touched the surface. In the dream something would explode inside me too, and I would go running away across a green field. Maria had adopted her son when he was seven, she was saying, and he had no interest in football. She was attempting the age-old experiment of making a different kind of man, so she was sending him to Emotional Class. I think Grandpa is not in touch with his emotions, the boy said thoughtfully, because he left the room in abrupt silence once and then returned to give the boy a pack of M&M's. But M&M's were an emotion.

Forty years ago many men were named Nuno. Now nobody was. Nuno had hardened his heart at the age of fifteen because he had become too emotional about football. Who could bear it, for more than a season? It was not possible, you had to grow up and become a wolfman, and write a dissertation about Pessoa's heteronyms. Now he could not feel anything about the games. What would happen if you allowed it? we asked, and he answered, and we explained that we had just taken him to Emotional Class. Nuno laughed, and closed his mouth quickly again. The thing glowed so greatly in the place of the night. He checked his phone; he had to leave, to go to a restaurant where the president always ate after meeting his mistress, and where spectators gathered in groups to watch.

Friends, he said, when Maria asked; you don't know them. You have friends I don't know? she said. Who?

It was our names coming toward us, Teresa and I had said, and the sudden sight of our own faces, and the way your nape would sometimes prickle as you turned a page. People would grab me and say I love you, Teresa said, but you don't love me, you don't know me. But maybe one or two of them really did. Maybe that was how the president had met his mistress, she had simply come up to him in the street one day and handed him all the candy she had.

Not a big deal, Nuno said wonderfully. He had said the same thing about reviewers who talked too much about your hair; that couldn't be the thing that kept you from leaving your house. But Maria and I knew better. You could get trapped in there for years, writing biographies of objects. Nuno rose. The game was over, or he would watch it on the way. He would keep his hair forever; he was fifteen years old. In Paris, there would be lithographs and strange old prints everywhere: of hands into paws, elongate faces, greater hunger; the transformation of a creature into a human being.

The Ranking of the Arts

What made Paris look like Paris? It was the absence of the Eiffel Tower, who peeped and hid, peeped and hid. Up and down the Avenue de la Bourdonnais I swept, like a spore, in the massive hypebeast shoes I was wearing for some reason. Every article of clothing I had packed was so ugly. I listened to music and wept, it was spring. I was lonely for everyone I had ever known.

Thinking of you, I wrote to my normal friend, and your residency four years ago. But I am here, she said, next week, in Paris. We would meet, at the place I would never go on my own, between old-ivory and low-crowned buildings. I put three miniature French apples in my bag, one for each of us and one for her husband, which, though we were starving by the end of things, would not be remembered, would never be shared out.

Of course I haven't seen a rhino, she said, amazed, as we waited in line outside the Musée d'Orsay. Why have *you* seen a rhino? There were only two zoos in her entire country. Well, as children, we used to spend the night there, I told her. With the nocturnal animals, the brimming eyes in the dark, the bats folded in thirds like black letters. The bars. The *behavior*—and I described to them my cubicle at the Library, where I was locked in as an exhibit, and labeled with my species. But too, I had just seen a taxidermied one at Deyrolle, head and bust only, like a president.

Three days ago the prime minister had resigned, possibly because of a letter she had written. I told them my gossip of the president of Portugal, that it was said he had a mistress in a district where he went to eat spaghetti and meat pies every night. Spaghetti and meat pies? No one ordered that. This was exactly how regional specialties were born. In fifteen years it would be on every menu—O Presidente, that was just how it happened.

The subject of her books was often: What if there were three? In our odd number, and a blaze of paint, we strode into the museum. It was night, and said to be the emptiest time, and everyone was there. Neither of us spoke of a belief that this would return things—to what? *The Origin of the World* had been removed for loan. (Subject: Woman, Vulva; Period, Realism.) But even on the brochure you could see—the hair like a scene of crisp weather, and at the top of her thigh, the little oyster that was only ever seen in person. That was what realism was, the thing that was there and almost no one ever painted.

"Everyone loves the Impressionists," my husband often said darkly—leaving no question what he thought of them, the photorealistic cow lover. Because of him I knew the mechanics of an exhibit, that someone chose the colors and painted the walls, someone wrote the awful copy, someone hung the masterpieces. Because of him I knew of *the basement*, where a thousand other pieces slept in the subconscious and awaited their time. He had just been laid off—because of the Rothkos, I explained, how he had poured, and also because recently they had superheated his museum, with a large silver-foil inflatable butterfly sculpture. Apparently none of the management had ever played God with a magnifying glass and a line of ants. It was our lives, but I loved to tell this part: The thing was called *Earth Angel*, and when the sun struck it . . .

We climbed upstairs and looked out on the Seine through the glass of a great going clock. There were the sunflowers, horrible. There was his ball lightning rolling through haystacks. There was the yellow bedroom, third of its kind—you could paint nothing but bedrooms everywhere you went. Could be sick. Could rest. Could sleep. "Before that I knew well enough that one could fracture one's legs and arms and recover afterwards, but I did not know that you could fracture the brain in your head and recover from that too. . . ."

And did you go mad? I asked shyly. Remembering her escape from the country, four years ago, and just before the borders closed. I thought it would join a circle together, to see her again. But no, she said, just in the normal way. It was the overgrowth of pattern, I told her. Time was compound, was the water droplet, and all human speech was refrains, to ring. A hyperobject, a Louis Wain cat, I said, when anyone asked what I was doing. The challenge was to find a new style for a material reality. Because there was something to it, this idea that maybe Monet just couldn't see that well.

She liked paintings of things scattered on mantelpieces. I liked empty bottles tipped in front of mirrors, and ateliers, and eels. Man do I go for eels, I often thought, standing in front of a still life. I liked the cream concentricities of pearls, with one lick of wild blue or lilac in the center. Often in an atelier, someone naked was standing, while others simply went around their business. How would you describe the look on her face? she asked, of the little bare courtesan. But the word, I knew, must be in French, staring out between her earrings. I watched your interview, my teacher would tell me when I returned, to see if you were wearing anything you had made.

I liked a badly rendered animal in someone's lap, and orange rinds. I liked, in *Starry Night over the Rhône*, a color that was almost annealing: deep dark inside an abalone shell. "But the painter of the future will be *a colourist such as has never yet existed*." Possibly I had been too long in Paris; I was lonely for people who hadn't been born yet. It was beautiful last week, I kept repeating—imagine saying that to one of Berthe Morisot's babies. It was blue just before you were here, and crystal, and everything holding its breath. Paris was convinced I had a child—a crib next to the bed in my hotel room, and I would not have it taken away.

A person's life was in her neck, I thought, the great axis, upon which balanced the vision of things. We were afraid of each other— of each other's gifts—and often found ourselves in the same cities without knowing, and once or twice a year had dreams, mine about little chauns in the countryside, hers about McDonald's. Or perhaps the fear was of being born different. Certainly I would rather have been an emotional genius, and able to pull people out of air. Her soft raining atmosphere all round. One strand of hair escaping like the first drop of dye in water. How she had managed, like the world in those early shutdown days, to keep having the dream in which everyone was there.

I wanted to ask if she had become afraid of her name. I wanted to ask if she had noticed the new grammar, like people falling down spiral staircases. But turned away from her, the acrylic observer, and allowed myself to become lost in my hypebeast shoes, until I came round the corner and saw her again, looking very long at a portrait by an Irish painter. I took a picture of her looking—a sin against her nature. She was, as I saw her, a series of pink pivots. And how, she asked me, turning neatly on one ankle, *do you rank the arts?*

FILM

I am not sure why I mentioned it first. I watched in such a way that my vision would sometimes open on a human face, so that the whole thing was broken into alps and folded napkins and swirls of spread cream cheese; that was Marlene Dietrich, last time it had happened. NOT TRUE! I ALWAYS HATED CATS! she had written in an unauthorized biography of herself, which the Library kept in a box of treasures and tenderly showed me first thing when I showed up. It had broken on the face of Shakespeare's wife, suddenly free from the zoo of her films, as she told me how we would do it in the movie: *It's simple. We build an animatronic baby with a lamp for its head*, as her loveliness lifted from her neck and floated, as my heart began to plummet through strange levels of art.

DANCE

We agreed that dance would be high, if we ever saw any in person. Actually Jamie, my dancer friend, had come with me for the first week of my stay. At the Airbnb, on matching sofa beds—with one of her boobs sometimes out, for the Dance—we talked into the small hours about the Six Viewpoints. Space story time emotion movement shape. I spoke of my cubicle downstairs at the Library, where I was displayed to the people, next to a sign printed with my name. A perfect opportunity for performance art; we began to spitball ideas. That I would slowly dress or undress, or cook a little meal on a doll's stove, or hang my laundry, or pull an Abramović and invite them in to do things to me. I locked my notebook in when I left—a thrill, like leaving my arm or leg—to see if anything happened to it overnight. But why leave at all? I could sleep on the floor. I could burst through the glass. I could buy that weird baby doll in the shop on Rue Cler that appeared to scream while extending Jesus fingers, and hold it.

COSTUME

Anything can be dance, can be performance, I thought, as Jamie broke new movement into the stillness—as she strode through the Tuileries and into Serge Lutens, to try a perfume that described itself as "fruity floral *and insane*." She dabbed me with it before the 1920s-themed party the Library was throwing, which had been a source of great stress to my mind as I packed. How twenties should I be? I wondered, searching the shops before finally finding a period headpiece with a real bird talon on it, nearly as painful to wear as it must have been for the bird. "Now here," Jamie said, "this is how the Charleston goes," and that was painful too. Before the party there was a dinner, at which a man named Bertrand in full tuxedo kept cleverly gathering to himself all the rolls. The theme, as it always did now, exploded into the night. Black feathers all over the bathroom. A former Miss America sang very, very low. Bertrand recently had his feet removed, his most loving wife explained, tall, with her hair like the torch of the Statue of Liberty, as she took my arm and accompanied me downstairs and to the dance floor.

THE LECTURE

I had been asked to speak about the portal—its language, its trajectory, whether it had died—but I had left it long ago. Well, day by day, in secret, I followed the progress of the poster who had had an apparent stroke. Inversions, absurdities, careful derangements of grammar and spelling—these had been his domain. They were his domain now. A coarse line of staples down the center of the scalp, looking just like the ones I recognized, had tended. Any damage to the human body now seemed so personal. I so excited, he posted one day, terrible Comedy Its about to dropped. He was getting well then, I thought, one way or the other, but TWITTER EST MORT, I wrote on the whiteboard.

COLLABORATION

It was Paris, it was spring, we were meant to be in love, and instead we had a ranking of the arts. I have a contract with the light, Anne Carson said, to describe it every morning. And the light, without my glasses, was my only lens. The faces passed me like thumbprints, people I knew, for everyone was here for the Olympics.

The waiters are racing tomorrow, Missy told me. The cubicle next to mine was reserved for her and Royce, composers who had the good sense never to be there, for in the building there were neither ghosts nor Wi-Fi. They were like celestial twins, twinkling together along one shared constellational wall, and were constantly trying to get opera ideas. No, they weren't to be had in the basement of the Library, but out in the city, abroad in the streets, where the shadows fell like latte art. Their first one, they told me, had been *Breaking the Waves*. I had sort of forgotten what happened in *Breaking the Waves*: a Skarsgård laid up from an oil rig incident, and his wife had to go out and fuck the world? But finally it would make sense; it would be sung. I glanced back and forth between the two. I kept mixing up who was in charge of the music, and who made the next thing happen. There was that news story I had clipped recently, about a woman who mixed up her twins: *Each of them was glad that they were not the other*. They searched the air around me for librettos; I loved it. There were other forms of insanity, besides mine.

OPERA

How long is your wand? we asked the conductor, sitting outside Les Deux Magots—cold enough for blankets, and the sun somewhere going down. And how had Hemingway had it, in his big loopy script? Get to a place where you can go on the next day. Do that every time. The conductor drew the straw out of his Art Deco and showed us the proper movement—without moving the wrist, or drawing big blossoms like poor Tár. No, he had not watched Bradley Cooper as Leonard Bernstein; he had seen too much tape of the man for that. Who cuts the hair of conductors? His was like fraque, black and swept back; the thing he refused to wear on his body, because *it meant some-*

thing 110 years ago but no longer means anything now. Serious, he was serious. Certain fake bitches—he did not say—wanted to have like jewels all over theirs, but his was thirty-three centimeters, and it sleeps at home.

His wife was a premier Carmen who was aging out of the Carmen role. In pictures her creamy arms and shoulders seemed vigorous beyond belief—from swirling her skirts, like the frills of snails, during the habanera. And what will she do next? I asked, my heart in the balcony. He took a deep breath, it was serious, I think it will be Wagner. This was the only adult conversation I had ever had in my life. Your voice could get bigger, this happened to people, and not fit inside the death scene anymore. It seemed natural to look at him, long and intensely, and to follow the white marble movement of his hands. In such a way what was happening could be an opera. Some directors tried to hide the conductor, but watching that figure was part of it for me. It's all part of it, he said, your seats, whether you can see the left side of the stage. He had once been to see a play where the performers went into the audience—this changed my life, he said. A whole planet of actors, who all got too big for Carmen, stepping off the stage and into the night.

COURTSHIP

Leave off in the middle of a sentence, if you have to. Leave something for the morning, so it will come. The waiter placed a square of chocolate in front of me and only me. I thought that was very cute, said the conductor: an observer of gesture, of timing. Are you racing tomorrow? Missy turned to ask the waiter; she was going to go watch them at eight a.m. No, he said, *that one over there—but he's too old, not fast, he will not win*. His lips shaped from birth by the word *bah*. She tried to pay him, but he had already been paid. *The wine is good*, he asked her softly, *no?* Then—it must have been an opera because in a moment of madness, they gripped and held each other's arms.

MARRIAGE

The Eiffel Tower, some time past, had been married and divorced. In the hotel room next to mine, the unseen man with the temper. "What do you want?" he yelled, time and again. *"What do you fucking want?"* The voice seemed to ricochet among my apples and oranges. "I want a husband who doesn't scream curses at me!" the wife cried out finally, and for a while after that there was silence: mine too.

Probably that man would live forever. This is the law I often thought of in conjunction with my father: A Bastard Lives Forever—whereas my husband was now expected to die just whenever. But not you, he told me fondly. A Lockwood through and through. Why not? I always said to Heidi, when she asked how I would feel about some particular change. In the show, he would be Latino, I would have a bedwetting problem, and we would be polyamorous and sleep with carnival workers.

What do you want? What do you fucking want? "My thin crescent-destiny seemed to enlarge." A full moon that night, but I could not find it. Maybe my life was meant for her. Maybe the crib was supposed to be theirs. Maybe I would soak the bed that night. Who knew?

TRANSLATION

Mornings I worked at the Bleu Olive. There was a newer café next door, NOIR—a coworking space with seats like mushrooms, full of adult burlap babies. I rejected this from the bottom of my soul, not least because I could hear my husband's classic pronunciation of it in my head: Nuahhh. I sat by the door, where there were fewer voices and where the rain came in, and pronounced *double espresso* so wrong I almost cried. The second one was easier, I would raise one finger; *a duck drank it*, like Teresa.

I knew that cotton candy was *Daddy's beard*. I knew a crazy word for pussy: *crougnougnous*. But where was grammar, where were pronouns, where the gender of a table? When I was finished I would hand back my cup, then trudge back along Rue Cler in my hypebeast shoes, regretting my high school French, which had vanished so completely. Once I found myself walking behind a dapper old man who had a large green beetle crawling through the white swoops of his hair. It was having a momentous journey, and kept catching Anne Carson's light, but this was part of the human contract: No matter how American, how full of processed cheese you are, you can't just let an old man have a bug on his head. I stepped toward him, saying softly, L'insecte! Scarabée! And lifted it with a tissue, and set it free on a quivering stem, only later thinking, *Oh God what if I had crushed it?* What are the high school words that will rise to you, in the necessary moment! Mon Dieu, the man kept laughing, Mon Dieu!

NAVIGATION

Go! John urged me, and pushed me across the street, into the car with the passionate taxi driver. "You stay young forever," the man told me, whipping around moodily, "because you look good." And drew a meditative face with his hand over his face, as finally, I caught the Eiffel Tower sparkling out the window. "Kind," he said to himself, "you seem kind. I speak English to you," he said, "because you make me dream."

THE INTERVIEW

Who is interviewing you? they had asked me in Lisbon, and he was, according to them, the cruelest man alive, who had personally called their friends fat virgins in print. Don't worry, I said, I will take revenge on him for you, and for all the fat virgins of Portugal! I sat down at the conference table and took a hateful sip of water, and crossed my arms hard over the apples in my jacket. But when he showed up he was a little boy, with a dense coal-black crew cut, and he smiled a great deal with his face tipped up like a sunflower. Nervous— leaping here and there like a landscape, geese rising off the water. He talked about Pina Bausch, *The Rite of Spring*, and I leaned forward and said that was in my book, and I talked about how she seemed able to make decisions all the way down to the hem of her hair. I knew then that he could not be the cruel man. "I thought that was a wonderful conversation, didn't you?" he burst out at the end, as we walked past the scale model of the museum we were in, and I said I thought it was. Before he left he showed me how cheek kissing was done. Two in Portugal, left side, right side, and never let them tell you it's three in France, that's too much.

POETRY

Now we will have a ranking of the arts. I gave up poetry, Teresa had said, now I am just my name. But one of my husband's medicines was making him write poetry again, for the first time in twenty years. Art must be a relay—I had taken over for him, all that time, now perhaps he would take over for me. So while I sat in my cubicle reading *A Walking Tour in Southern France*, or turned delicately through the dried-petal pages of *Harmonium*, he would send me new phrases he had discovered, such as "a rascal of crab" and "a clock where her body circles the hours like hands . . ." not knowing what I stared through, out of the museum and over the Seine.

It also caused him to write new Beatles songs. One was called "John's the Hippopotamus."

> *Cobras eat cantaloupes*
> *And cantaloupes eat antelopes*
> *And antelopes eat cormorants*
> *The hipp-o-pot'mus said*

But writing new Beatles songs was easy; all it required was a proper name and a nonsense element. "Macready's Marmalade Register," "Mr. Tolstoy, You're Driving Me Mad," try it. I shared with him some of my fresh Beatles knowledge—that in the Soviet Union, they used to scratch the grooves of the records into discarded X-ray plates and play them that way. No, I had no idea how that worked either, but it sounded so fucking good.

What are you working on? I could ask him that again. For the last nine days, he told me, he had been writing a poem called "Superheated Museum." "And everywhere you touched," the last line went, "a garden opened." He was thinking of getting a tattoo, of long flowers on the scar.

BIOGRAPHY

The cruelest man in Lisbon was the one who would describe your hair in the first paragraph, make it impossible for you to live. But it was lyrical, where she had put it up against the window. Outside, in the first green, and what the Portuguese considered cold, two teens were teaching each other capoeira. Well, one of them had to take the lead, and show the other exactly how slow.

This was the first conference of its kind, they claimed. My event was coming—who had I written a biography of? Whose face would be projected on the huge screen behind me? If all else failed, I calculated, I could say things about Virginia Woolf's heart problems. But: *Yours*, Teresa informed me afterward, and your name crossed out in red. And the record-keeper ruby began to glow from its gold.

But first, the Beatles, who went on longer than dunes. Their biographer climbed the steps to the stage and you saw at once that he was in hell, for there would always be another fact, another quote, a living witness—I offer you a little scene, an old man in the audience said, half rising, they rigged up a radio between two chimneys, in the days of the dictatorship, and the old man would listen, crouched on the floor, and *I think it was the most beautiful thing I ever heard in my life*, though maybe he said the *most beautiful days*, and I was starting to weep, perhaps Teresa was, and the biographer was becoming desperate, he couldn't deal with yet another *most beautiful thing*, where would it all fit, what was he writing, the Bible? And would he ever finish, other people of the past were worried, because we are the ones who were there, we are the ones who remember, and the biographer began to panic, white pages rose over his head, he had even made a promise to read the manuscript to someone on his deathbed. And I may die, he acknowledged, before the biography is finished, but someone has to get it right, someone has to tell it how it happened: And there it was, another most beautiful day, someone coming to take the microphone, and what the old man was going to say—the music—still hanging in the air.

Epilogue

Billie and I stayed after class one week, talking with the teacher about the glimpse. I'm getting chills! we kept exclaiming, and showing each other our forearms. It was live performance for me, I said, any kind, bad or good, people working together to make something, a reality, ribbons through the shoulders of dancers. But the teacher surprised me. It was, she said, when she could see the line under a painting, the pencil. She rolled her eyes a little. *Then* I feel like, now I'm really seeing something. The bar of light leading you on through the city, the line of story, the scar. In Paris I had almost seen it, people tearing into baguettes on the street with their teeth, children disappearing around corners with their instruments. You like the glimpse through the hedge, I said then, and we all shivered and held out our arms, and, Good title for a book, Billie said, laughing.

That was the artist's hand, I told them, up at the podium, a teacher myself. It is the evidence that once you make something it stays made. Now someone was asking about the ending, how you knew—but the end was an oasis you never wanted to reach. The best version was when you were in it and all the components were in hurricane. No one could ever read that but you and the people who inherited your papers, but it was the real thing, in its way. If I could communicate the way it was put together, or the act of putting-togetherness. This was a kind of immortal life. "Her body was to be found—her correct body and mind were to be found—in the process of assembly."

As usual I was there as a kind of traveling exhibit. I showed up to the student gathering and immediately screamed, Like a seagull, they're lying to you! Which they were, whoever they were. They were calling it a demitasse but there wasn't even coffee, let alone the little cups. They were selling glamour to children, but look where I had been put: a hotel with a clam-themed bathroom, though possibly all bathrooms were clam-themed for me now. I ran a palm down the side of my face. One of the students was wearing the hugest pants possible, big enough to conceal anything. I said, You must go out to the jungle, the deep wood, the night cove. All that sounded very impressive. "The clam zone."

What I was telling them was to invent a cryptid, something to be seen. It must be the most regional thing on earth. With Chey, who was from Iowa, I invented the Cob, who was like Jesus with a row missing, and had butter running in hot rivulets down him. Chey wrote plays in which narcolepsy featured as a formal device, and in fact had written one during lockdown where the protagonist kept waking to new spotlit circumstances, like me and my mother during that drive down Route One, slipping in and out of sleep to new worlds. It was so strange, Chey said, their roommate had the window and it wasn't like you could just ask—for a slice of the window, a taste, a rotation. The roommate was a theater major and had to take a three-hour Zoom call in the middle of every day, which called up those stethoscopes of Jamie's and the six-feet-apart hearts, actors trying to keep the whole human comedy alive in incubators. You don't want to remember now, I said, as Chey shivered, but write it all down, you will want it later, you will want everything later.

My own cryptid was MANGRO, but I did not speak of him to the students. I had encountered him on a birthday trip to the Florida Keys, prepared to turn, as I had done for the last few years, the secret number between two and three. Instead the dizziness, the arching backward of the neck, the long ungrammatical fall down nautilus stairs—all disappeared, as if they suddenly couldn't find me. The first morning I woke and felt no presences, heard no voices, saw no souls rise in curves from other people's heads. On the TV, a drag queen was being Reba, the surest possible sign of order in the universe. "And I'm MEXICAN!" he exclaimed. "But I just love to do her." Oh, was I well? Was it simply the island? My husband proposed an experiment: to drive north up the bridge toward Miami and see where it started to happen. The eccentric guidebook, neon as a gobi, rested on my lap, growing warm in the sun like its original tree. I rolled the window down. And there he was: MANGRO, a tangle among mangrove roots, dragging his accumulation through the key-lime water.

You didn't know what would be important, I had understood in Scotland. At the Fairy Pools we bought one nephew a stuffie of Nessie wearing a plaid beret that he carried around constantly for the next five years. Everyone was always trying to throw it away or wash it, but his whole life now was organized around the search: for that thing to hold on to, that line rising into a neck. This is the imposition of form, I told the students. Out of the first string, a knotted thing. What had emerged from the first ooze but a tangle. Something submerged saying *this* is like *that*. Two legs a metaphor for movement in the world. And light was too light, it needed a name.

MANGRO could not become endangered, he was a glimpse. Actually, he was climbing more northward every year. Two scientists had tracked him through the wetlands, and had to keep going and going. In his mind, fluorescing emeralds. The line from the eccentric guidebook, "Together they grasp the twig . . ." about the mating of roseate spoonbills. The woman who wrote it was an animal jaw flying a strip of tan skin. She was a contemporary but I no longer feared her. Why had I feared my contemporaries? Because they were alive and I was not. I was supposed to get an award with her—a prize for being able to read—after my husband almost exploded on the plane, but we awoke in a capsule hotel that morning and thought, What on earth are we doing here? Go home.

She always wore dark sunglasses. "You know what its flesh feels like?" she had asked of that other intelligence, the octopus. "Like the inside of your cheek." When I thought of her getting the award I saw her stealing the gold bar out of Mel Fisher's treasure museum, though I never imagined them calling me forward, or me stumbling up the aisle alone.

"The Shark is not in the Tarot," she had written. It was a fine guidebook, really too fine. You could open it at any moment and be back there, with little drawings. And she was right. That was the best place to watch the sunset. That was the best beach in all the keys, where I picked up a pebble that looked like a manatee with a boat scar. She lived there, as a MANGRO sighter, and had put her mother's

Alzheimer's into her books. She was why I was going to give it up—a bad review had put her off for ten years, and she was never so feral again, she said. And what was it worth, the criticism of a person who might wake up any given morning unable to speak English? So that it had become impossibly precious, a disappearing and reappearing gold bar.

"She's a keeper," Joy had written of the baby who couldn't be aborted. I was really, really confused about changelings, I thought. Her characters said Hello, the tree, when they saw a tree and Hello, rug, when they came into a room. They brought each other little stones from places. What she liked was the line about us all being changed in the twinkling of an eye—that line was everywhere, like the hope for it. She would write, with a straight face, "His name was Drawdy." She would say, with her animal jaw, "Jesus walked out." All through the keys were little legends that had made their way into her work. Even:

On This Site
In 1865
Nothing
Happened

The new cats at the Hemingway house were interlopers. A Polish man, red-faced and breathing heavily, flung himself against the grille of the writing studio, as if the outside world were a jail and he needed to be let in: to write letters to his readers, throw crumpled paragraphs into the elephant's foot trash can. He jostled me aside; I held the key without knowing it. Out of green jealousy—for I was alive, and still working—Hemingway ate two of my dollars, in the form of the malfunctioning Coke machine.

No longer magnetized to the wind and weather. No longer wanted, for the moment, by death. In this place your hand could not be larger than your hand, your face could not detach and go floating, you could not be standing six inches to the side of yourself, your foot could not be "too far away." Yet what a thing it had been, to observe from outside myself. What ink in the bloodstream had persisted? What part of me, throughout, had still tried to depict? I drew a picture of MANGRO and gave him large clear goggling eyes. MANGRO was a thought, a big connected thought. The sunlight was his consciousness. He trailed along outside the ark, making conversation with the open-mouthed barnacles. The line of poetic logic, I explained to the students, is as easy to disrupt as the narrative; *is* the narrative, where none appears to exist. The line, healed purple, went straight through the notebook, which no one had asked me to keep. The pathetic diary, Sontag's Quentin had called it—a relic to be reread later or left unread as a luxury, like white chocolate. But that's what I did, my husband told me. I meant to tell you, in the hospital. I asked you to take those pictures *so I would be there to look at them later.*

On our return, a long upchuck in the aisle like Mel Fisher's discovery of the treasure. A teenage soccer player looked down at his lap and found himself suddenly rich, and a temporary mother had to take him off the plane to clean him. That was just what life was like now, we understood. A massage therapist had recently thrown up on my sister's face, when she had gone there with her grief group. They were all bereaved mothers but one of the women had had two separate children murdered, so . . . "If it had to be one of us, I'm glad it was me," my sister said, shrugging. There was a deadpan above deadpan, on the heavenly plane. "I dreamed of that infant for some years," Williams had written. "I'm told I wasn't exactly well during that period, but the things I could see!" Are you Joy? I might have said that morning, to a pair of sunglasses on the great headache. I have been saving you my whole life, I might have told her that day.

The morning I transcribed my notes about MANGRO my husband came upstairs as I was in the whirl of it, to keep me in that moment that was the making. I saw ahead of me an afternoon—an island with one palm tree, where I might keep filling in details until it was solid enough to live on. My island, where I slept, ate, found shade. Was naked, like Crusoe, but still had pockets. We mapped a route to Saint Helena and from there to Hunting Beach, an out-of-the-way state park. Nearby was rumored to live an eleven-foot-long alligator named King Arthur, who was *forty years old* and had recently been "crowned with a tomato cage," because even the primordial swished with us in the pageant. And I'm an alligator! I thought. But I just love to do her.

Immediately the beach was strange: Six steps and you were in the water, which thrashed as if huge gray-green mermaids, down at the foundations of the world, were churning it. Wave after slapping wave. Not even the surfers had anticipated it. Just a few children, lying ecstatically on their boogie boards at the first break in the water, waiting for the pure interval to lift them. Which it always did.

The distance, off to the right, looked different. We walked a little ways past the people and civilization ceased. The sand bucked up and dropped us—a blacktop road broken up and abandoned, even a little red fire hydrant gone feral to one side. Things went whiter and whiter in waves, until you could imagine your own bleached knucklebone being used in some future game of chance. Pelicans in floating lines like pterodactyls, and the sound of the wind like something already in the body. I stood still and looked; for once I really was the center. A whole forest surrounded me, dead and touched to silver, like long platinum ponytails combed out and hanging upward.

And he was everywhere. The whole place was a cathedral to MANGRO. Standing spires, exposed intricate roots, free-range pews and uncompleted arches, all breathing through the tiniest pinholes. Had it been this way forever? I asked, clambering up and over the trunks. Only for the last twenty years. The live silver of the driftwood couldn't be captured in photographs—but I could describe it, the white spotlight under the flame, votives flickering without fire. Someone had even built a twig- and palm-roofed shelter, of the ideal kind I had imagined. At the entrance, a pine cone levitating in a ray. Jason took a picture of me sitting cross-legged there. I had never looked larger in my life.

So what is MANGRO's deal exactly? he asked. But in the process of assembly you couldn't say too much. I groped my way back inside the whirlwind of paper, the description coming in short pants. He's like a thought—or a light on the mind—he reveals. Not a piece of scenery but the person behind it. Looks like a tangle, but that's our un-understanding. All connections necessary. Not something wrong with the brain. The brain itself. I opened up the notebook (which I had brought like my family) to show.

There was a name for this place that we wouldn't know till later—boneyard beach. They were trying to save the lighthouse through the placement of something called groins, with the result that the southern end was being sucked faster and faster into the sea. Everyone says the same thing: that it is like going into the past. *Deep* past, where marriages between teenagers took place "in a green tropical forest in the time of the dinosaurs." It looks like the lost world—not the one we lost through our own carelessness, but another. "Large rustic brick fireplace or stone fireplace in a cabin . . . the logs that were in front of the fireplace transformed into raspberries and now the raspberries are transforming into fire ants . . . now I'm inside the movie *Breakfast at Tiffany's* and I'm walking up the stairs and now I'm on the Eiffel Tower looking down, there's a man parachuting down the middle of the Eiffel Tower . . . now I see battleships, like a fleet of battleships charging across the ocean . . . and I see . . . Sherwood Forest."

My earrings whipped like stone pages. We were perfectly happy. The parasailor and the striped umbrellas and the quiet picnics were folded into shimmering sheets behind us; when the line was broken, there was left only the layering, air upon air upon air, I told the students. Ahead of us went MANGRO'S priests, the only other living people in a prehistoric world. A boy's hair in soft spirals. A woman covered in white from head to toe. My husband took his shirt off, unmindful of the scar, which in this context of long weathering just looked like an event—as if a tree surgeon might indicate that particular ring and say: Something happened here. I thought again of his crisscrossing nexus in the hospital. It was true that you couldn't unsee afterward. Where does MANGRO live? he asked me. Well, in water. And in the corner of the eye.

Did a thing to be glimpsed—health, illness, sanity—maintain its solidity from moment to moment? MANGRO rippled through the water; his whole life was his power to disturb. At least it looked that way to us. Something in the brain, neurofibrillary. An amyloid plaque. A protein called Tau—wasn't that wonderful? Birds nested in him. Silver swam through his legs. Kayakers traded tales of him. Like someone in a cartoon, he picked up his bush and walked.

> *I prayed, he said*
> *Who did you pray to?*
> *Ganesh, Christian god, ancestors*
> *Oh, I did Jah, too*
> *World mother? Gaia*
> *Also aliens*

Pay attention to the first place you cut yourself, the teacher told us, for you will always cut yourself in the same place again. But now the light did nothing, the rain did not rain me, no souls rose in bright curves from the tops of people's heads. Still, someone in the crowd must be able to see it: We had walked all the way out of the world. And come back. I stood at the podium and pointed, a Band-Aid on my first finger. My blood pouring highlighter on a line in the neon guidebook: that *fish would use disasters as temporary reefs.*